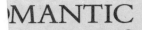

ROMANTIC
SUSPENSE

Sparked by Danger, Fueled by Passion.

Cowboy Deputy
by
CARLA CASSIDY

Following a run of bad luck, including an attack
on her grandfather, Edie Tolliver is sure things
can't possibly get any worse....

But with the handsome Deputy Grayson on the
case will Edie's luck and love life turn a corner?

LAWMEN
of BLACK ROCK

*Available January 2011
wherever books are sold.*

Visit Silhouette Books at www.eHarlequin.com

SRS27709

KAREN WHIDDON

Colton's Christmas Baby

ROMANTIC
SUSPENSE

Special thanks and acknowledgment to
Karen Whiddon for her contribution to
The Coltons of Montana miniseries.

SILHOUETTE BOOKS

Recycling programs
for this product may
not exist in your area.

ISBN-13: 978-0-373-27706-3

COLTON'S CHRISTMAS BABY

Visit Silhouette Books at www.eHarlequin.com

Printed in U.S.A.

Books by Karen Whiddon

Silhouette Romantic Suspense

One Eye Open #1301 ★
One Eye Closed #1365 ★
Secrets of the Wolf #1397 ★
The Princess's Secret Scandal #1416
Bulletproof Marriage #1484
Black Sheep P.I. #1513 ★★
The Perfect Soldier #1557 ★★
Profile for Seduction #1629 ★★
Colton's Christmas Baby #1636

★*The Pack*
★★*The Cordasic Legacy*

Harlequin Nocturne

Cry of the Wolf #7 ★
Touch of the Wolf #12 ★
Dance of the Wolf #45 ★
Wild Wolf #67 ★

Signature Collections

Beyond the Dark
 "Soul of the Wolf"

KAREN WHIDDON

started weaving fanciful tales for her younger brothers at the age of eleven. Amidst the Catskill Mountains of New York, then the Rocky Mountains of Colorado, she fueled her imagination with the natural beauty of the rugged peaks and spun stories of love that captivated her family's attention.

Karen now lives in North Texas, where she shares her life with her very own hero of a husband and three doting dogs. Also an entrepreneur, she divides her time between the business she started and writing the contemporary romantic suspense and paranormal romances that readers enjoy. You can email Karen at KWhiddon1@aol.com or write to her at P.O. Box 820807, Fort Worth, TX 76182. Fans of her writing can also check out her website, www.KarenWhiddon.com.

To my three faithful writing companions,
Daisy Mae, Mitchell Thomas and Mac Macadoo.
These three dogs (two miniature schnauzers and one
boxer) have kept me company through so many books,
barely opening their eyes when I talk to myself
or pace as I try to figure out a scene.
I couldn't do it without them.

Chapter 1

Reeking of whiskey, cigar smoke and some fast woman's cheap perfume, Darius Colton barely resembled the dignified patriarch Damien Colton remembered from his youth. Glaring at his prodigal son with red-rimmed eyes, Darius's upper lip curled in derision as he pondered Damien's question.

It was a question that deserved to be answered. Cursing his bad timing, Damien elaborated. "I'd like to see the bank statements for my account."

"Are you questioning my word?" Darius snarled, his consonants slightly slurred.

"No." Damien crossed his arms. "But that money should have been earning interest the entire time I was in prison. Now you're telling me there's nothing left?"

"That's exactly what I'm telling you, boy." With a dismissive smile, Darius turned away, only to glance back over his shoulder. "You've got nothing."

Damien checked his rising temper, one of the many neat tricks he'd learned while incarcerated. Who knew it would serve him so well here in the outside world?

He kept his voice level. "I never signed anything authorizing you—or anyone else—to touch that money. I need an explanation. Hell, I deserve an explanation."

In response, his sixty-year-old, white-haired father let loose with a string of curses vile enough to make a sailor blush. Darius's face went red, then purple as he glared at his son with rage-filled eyes.

So much anger. So much hate.

Fists clenched, Damien waited it out. When Darius finally ran out of steam, Damien stepped back. "We'll talk about this again when you're sober," he said. "As soon as possible."

In the act of pouring another glass of Scotch, Darius turned on him so fast the expensive liquor sloshed all over his sleeve. He didn't appear to notice or care, so intent was he on giving his son what the Colton kids used to call the death stare. If looks could kill...

"You will not mention this to me again. The subject is closed."

"Later," Damien insisted. "I promise you we will discuss this later." He'd been saying this for months now. Enough was enough.

Though Damien halfway believed if he persisted, Darius would haul off and slug him, he'd been through hell and back already. Since the day he'd been set free and the prison gates had disgorged him, he'd known that no event life might have in store for him could ever be as heinous as the day he'd been convicted of a crime he hadn't committed.

None. Ever.

So Darius blustering and trying to tell him that he'd somehow lost a three-million-dollar inheritance didn't even compare. Especially since Damien didn't believe a word his dear old father said. He needed to talk to his brothers. And Maisie, he amended silently. All of them.

And quickly. Though he'd been home for three whole months, he hadn't seen this coming. When had the old man become so...unstable and deceitful? Something had to be wrong. Darius didn't need his son's money—he had enough of his own. But why lie? Round and round Damien's mind went, trying to adjust to what had just happened. Darius couldn't have stolen his inheritance. The money had to be here somewhere. All Damien had to do was find it.

Watching as his father, whiskey glass in hand, staggered from his office to the master bedroom suites, Damien was left frustrated and empty-handed, wishing he could punch something.

Gradually, sounds from the great room penetrated his consciousness. Christmas carols, rustling and clinking and talking and laughter. He remembered now—the family was gathering for the annual Colton family Christmas-tree-decorating ceremony.

When he'd been in prison he'd dreamt of this event. Now, he wasn't even sure he'd bother to attend. He really just wanted to head out to the barn and saddle up Duncan, his favorite quarter horse gelding, and ride out to the back pastures. As a matter of fact—

"Damien!" His sister Maisie, grinning like a gleeful small child, bounced into the room. "Come on! Hurry! Wes and Duke are bringing in the tree. Finn's getting the stand ready and checking the lights. Even Perry, Brand and Joan are here along with their families! It's picture-postcard perfect. Everyone wanted to be a part of decorating for your first Christmas back with the family!"

And just like that, Maisie had deftly lobbed the ball in his court. Now he had no choice but to join the others.

Nodding, he allowed her to grab his hand and lead him into the great room. Even with almost the entire family gathered, the huge room was cozy rather than crowded. A fire roared in the massive stone fireplace and box after box of glittering ornaments were spread all over the huge oak coffee table, along with numerous strands of white lights. The place looked like a scene from a holiday magazine. Homey, folksy and warm.

And he felt completely out of place.

As Damien entered, Maisie's teenaged son Jeremy threw open the back door, letting in a gust of cold air. "Here they are!" he shouted, grinning broadly.

Covered in a light dusting of snow, Damien's twin brother Duke appeared, half carrying, half dragging the bottom of a huge spruce tree. Wes Colton held up the top part of the tree, laughing and looking for his fiancée, Lily Masterson, who was helping Duke's fiancée, Susan Kelley, organize ornaments. Even Finn Colton had driven in from town. Their youngest brother had gotten engaged to Rachel Grant, who was helping him check the light strands.

It was, Damien thought sourly, a regular love fest in here. Damien couldn't help but notice how the three outside women took pains to try and include Maisie in their little group. To his surprise, Maisie seemed to be eating it up. A genuine smile of pure happiness lit up her face and put a sparkle in her aquamarine eyes.

Happy and festive, a perfect combination. Christmas carols played and there was homemade wassail simmering in a slow cooker on a table, along with various other goodies: Christmas cookies and fudge, dip and chips, and ribbon candy. Had they gone overboard for him? Damien wondered. Or was this the normal holiday celebration here at the Colton ranch these days?

Either way, they wanted to include him. He knew

he should feel touched, but instead he only felt empty. Everyone had paired off, it seemed. Everyone except Damien. Oh, and their stepmother, Sharon, who appeared to be single-mindedly focused on drinking an entire bottle of wine by herself. No one seemed to notice or mind Darius Colton's absence.

Wes, Duke and Finn lifted the huge tree into the stand while the women oohed and aahed. The children, belonging to various branches of the Coltons in town, chased each other and laughed. Damien took a step back, intent on beating a swift exit, but Maisie saw what he was up to.

"Come on." Grabbing his hand, she pulled him closer to the tree. "I'm sure the guys need your help, right boys?"

Amid a chorus of agreement, she left him, bouncing over to help the women with the ornaments. As he helped secure the tree in the stand, Damien felt his twin's gaze on him, though he refused to meet it.

This was no good. He planned to make a quick retreat as soon as humanly possible.

"What, not feeling too Christmassy?" His brother Wes, the town sheriff, punched him lightly in the shoulder. At Damien's questioning look, he shrugged. "It's written all over your face."

"Yeah, well it's been a long time." Damien's voice sounded raspy. Eyeing each of his brothers, he couldn't help but wonder if Darius had stolen their inheritance, too.

Underneath the sparkle and tinsel, there was something rotten and foul here on the Colton ranch.

"I've got to go," he told Duke, once the tree stood tall and straight and ready for the lights.

"Where to?" Glancing at his watch, his twin grimaced.

"I thought I'd ride out and check fences in the high pasture."

"Now? It's dark and snowing. That can wait for the morning."

Feeling increasingly uncomfortable, Damien tugged the collar of his shirt. "I've got to get out of here."

Instantly, Duke's teasing smile faded. "Are you all right?" he asked, low-voiced. "You're looking a little green."

"Green?" Damien scowled. He forced himself not to bolt. "I'll be fine as soon as I get some fresh air."

Duke nodded, but Damien knew his twin didn't understand. How could he, when he'd spent his entire life enveloped in the love of his family? It was Damien who was different, Damien who was the outsider.

A few steps and Damien stood in the foyer. Already, the sense of constriction had eased somewhat. But not enough. Since it was late and dark and snowing, instead of going for a ride, he'd head into town for a beer. His favorite watering hole, the Corner Bar, would be quiet and soothing.

The short drive took longer, due to the snow. But at least the streets were mostly deserted and his four-wheel-drive pickup handled the snow with ease. He parked, noting only two other vehicles in the lot.

Stepping into the Corner Bar, he glanced around the place appreciatively. Dark and quiet and mercifully short on holiday decorations, it was exactly what he needed after the festive frenzy at the family ranch.

Stepping up to the long, polished mahogany bar, he captured a barstool. "Kind of empty tonight."

"Sure is." Without being asked, Jake, the bartender, brought him a tall Coors Light.

"Business slow during the holidays?" Damien asked, taking a long drink, enjoying the light foamy head.

"Yeah, you're my only drinking customer," Jake said, wiping at the bar counter with a rag that once might have been white and now was a cross between gray and yellow. "Except for her, and all she's drinking is a Shirley Temple."

He pointed and for the first time Damien realized he wasn't entirely alone in the place as he'd first supposed. Eve Kelley, her skin glowing softly in the dim light, occupied the corner booth, which sat mostly in shadows. With her head bent over a notebook, her long blond hair hung in silky curtains on each side of her face.

"Eve Kelley," he mused, wondering why the girl who'd been the most popular in town was all alone.

"Yeah." Leaning forward, the other man groused. "She's been here an hour and she's not even drinking alcohol. That's her second Shirley Temple."

Intrigued, Damien studied her, wondering why she'd come to a bar yet didn't drink? A problem with alcohol? She'd certainly been a party girl back in the day. Back when he'd been a senior in high school, he and she had heated up the front seat of his Ford F150. She'd been pretty and popular and since she was a few years ahead of him in school, way out of his league.

Eve had been the only one in town who'd written him a letter while he'd been in prison. Though he'd never acknowledged it, he'd always wondered why.

"I'm going to join her," Damien told the bartender.

Though the other man didn't comment, he shook his head in disapproval. He probably thought, as did most of the people in Honey Creek, Montana, that Damien was tainted.

Crossing the room to where she sat, he willed her to look up and smile, or stare or something. Anything other than recoil in horror and disgust. Though he'd been back home almost three months, he could count on the fingers of one hand the number of people who didn't act as though he was a leper.

He made it all the way to her table without her noticing.

"Enjoying your Shirley Temple?"

When she did raise her head and meet his gaze, he saw her eyes were still the same long-lashed, sapphire blue he remembered.

"It's a seven and seven," she said, making him wonder why she bothered to lie. What did she care what he thought?

"Mind if I join you?"

A flash of surprise crossed her face, and then she lifted one shoulder in a shrug. "Suit yourself."

He slid into the booth across from her, taking another long drink of his beer. "Good. I missed that while I was in prison."

Stirring her drink absently, she nodded. "I imagine there are quite a few things you missed, aren't there?"

Since she asked the question with a very real curiosity, he felt himself beginning to relax for the first time in what felt like ages. When he'd been in prison, he would have slugged anyone who tried to tell him it'd be a hundred times more tense back home than in the joint, but in reality he thought more about running away than anything else. Except sex. He thought about that a lot. Especially now. Eve Kelley, with her long blond hair and T-shirt, instantly made him think of sex.

No doubt she wouldn't appreciate knowing that, so he kept his mouth shut, giving her a nod for an answer.

Leaning forward, she studied him. Her full lips parted, making him want to groan out loud. "What did you miss the most?"

A flash of anger passed and he answered truthfully.

"The feel of a woman, soft and warm, under me, wrapped around me."

Her face flamed, amusing him. But to give her credit, she didn't look away. "I guess I sort of asked for that, didn't I?"

"No, actually you didn't." Chagrined, he offered her a conciliatory smile. "I'm sorry. I think sometimes I've forgotten how to act in public."

"I guess that's understandable."

Finishing his beer, he signaled for another one. The bartender brought it instantly, setting it on the table without comment and removing the empty glass.

"My turn." He leaned forward. "Tell me, Eve Kelley. What are you doing all alone in a bar, nursing a Shirley Temple, with a snowstorm threatening?"

"I needed to get away." For a moment, stark desperation flashed in her expressive eyes, an emotion he could definitely relate to.

"Holidays aren't all they're cracked up to be, are they?"

She shook her head, sending her large hoop earrings swinging in that mass of long straight hair.

Glancing at her left hand and seeing no ring, he took another drink. "I'm guessing you're not married?"

"Nope."

"Divorced, then?"

"Never married. I guess I just didn't meet the right person." She sighed. "I've never really minded before, but the holidays can be tough on anyone, and it's worse when you're nearly forty and still alone. My mother is now on a matchmaker tangent. She's determined to marry me off or die trying."

Her voice contained such disgust, he had to laugh.

Watching him, her lovely blue eyes widened. "You should do that more often," she said softly. "It suits you."

"Makes me look less frightening," he replied, unable to keep the bitterness from his voice. "Isn't that what you mean?"

Now she was the one who laughed and when she did, her face went from pretty to drop-dead stunningly beautiful. He watched as the flickering light danced over her creamy skin, the hollows of her cheeks, the slender line of her throat, and ached. Damn, he'd been too long without a woman.

Talking to her had been a mistake.

Yet he couldn't make himself leave this train wreck.

"You aren't frightening. Not to me," she said softly. "I forgot how funny you are. At least you kept your sense of humor."

"Maybe," he allowed, studying her. Time had been kind to her. He remembered her as a tall, elegant athletic girl, one of the popular ones that every guy lusted after. She'd been a few years out of school, but that hadn't stopped them for getting together one hot August night at a party in someone's newly harvested field. Maybe because his life had all but stopped when he'd been sent to prison, but he remembered that like it was yesterday.

Hell, for him it *was* yesterday. Sometimes he felt like a twenty-year-old kid walking around in the body of a thirty-five-year-old man. Other times he felt like he was a hundred.

Tonight, it was refreshing to be with someone who didn't act as though he were fragile or dangerous, or both.

He lifted his glass, inviting her to make an impromptu toast. "To old friends."

With a smile, she touched her glass to his. "To old friends."

"You look good, Eve."

To his disbelief, she blushed again. "Thanks. So do you. It's surprising, but you're easy to talk to."

He laughed. "Do you always say exactly what you think?"

"No. Not always. I run a beauty shop here in town—Salon Allegra, have you seen it?"

"I don't get to town much."

"I see." She nodded. "After high school, I was going to go to college, but ended up attending beauty school instead. I worked at The Cut 'N' Curl for a long time. When Irene died, she left me the place. I fixed it up and renamed it."

"You never left Honey Creek?" he asked, letting his gaze sweep her face. "Didn't you ever want to live somewhere else, to get away?"

"Not really. I've traveled a bit, but it's so beautiful here. Where else can you have all this?" She made a sweeping gesture with her hand. "Mountains and valley and endless prairie. Big Sky Country."

Despite the contentment ringing in her voice, something seemed off. He couldn't put his finger on it, not exactly, but he'd bet dissatisfaction lurked underneath her complacent exterior. The Eve Kelley he'd known had been a bit of a wild child, not this staid, watered-down version sitting in front of him.

"But didn't you ever feel like you were missing out?"

She regarded him curiously. "On what? I don't like cities and crowds and pollution. I love the big open spaces. Honey Creek has all I need."

"Really?"

She thought for a moment. "Okay, sometimes I have to head into Bozeman or Billings to shop, but most everything I could want I can get here in town."

He dipped his chin, acknowledging her words but still watching her closely. "You don't get bored?"

"How could I? I have my family and friends, my business and my family's business. No other place could give me that. And the people are friendly."

"Ah, friendly. Maybe to you. Not to me."

"That both surprises me and doesn't. Even though everyone in town knows you didn't kill Mark Walsh, they're afraid of you."

She'd succeeded in shocking him. "Afraid of me? Why? I've done nothing to them."

"You've been in prison for fifteen years. That's bound to have changed you, made you...tough."

She licked her lips and he could tell she was speaking carefully. "Some of the people in town are really scared. They don't know what kind of person you are after all this time."

Incredulous, he stared. "Are you serious? I've lived here my entire life. They know me."

"They know who you used to be. Not the man you've become."

"What about you?" Nerves jangling inside him, he leaned forward. "Do I frighten you? Are you afraid of me?"

She swallowed. "Though part of you is dark and dangerous, I'm not frightened. Actually, you intrigue me."

As soon as she spoke, her face colored, making him grin. "I didn't mean that like it sounded. It wasn't a come-on, I swear."

"Too bad," he said lightly. Then, while she appeared to be still trying to absorb this, he raised his hand to signal the bartender.

"I'll have another. And bring the lady another one, too, whatever she's drinking."

Appearing relieved, Eve settled back in her seat.

"What was it like?" she asked. "What was it like, being in jail all those years for a crime you didn't commit?"

"What do you think it was like?" Though he kept his tone light, he could feel the darkness settling over his face. "Being there was no picnic."

"I'm sorry."

"Don't be. He waved away her apology. "I'd wonder, too, if our situations were reversed."

"And now? What are you going to do now?"

Their drinks arrived, saving him from answering her question right away. He waited until the bartender had moved away, drinking deeply before meeting her gaze.

"I'd like to buy my own spread. Maybe in Nevada or Idaho. I'm not sure. But I can't stay with my family forever."

"Why not? We're going to be family soon, you know, since your brother Duke is engaged to my sister Susan. She said they're moving to his place on the ranch."

"She's there at the main house right now, decorating the Colton family tree."

"And you're not."

Instead of answering, he shrugged.

"You know, I don't understand why you'd want to leave Honey Creek. Your life is here, your heritage. Why would you want to throw all that away?"

When she looked so passionate, her blue eyes glowing, he wanted to kiss her. Hell, he wanted to do much more than that, but he'd settle for a kiss for now.

"Kind of personal, isn't it?" he drawled, leaning back in the booth.

"Come on, it's not that personal. It's not like we're complete strangers. I've known you forever. I've always envied what you have, that connection to the land."

He studied her. "You're right about that. I do love the

land, my family's ranch. If I could stay there, out on the land, and never have to deal with my father or with the town, that'd be one thing."

"You really dislike Honey Creek, don't you?"

He noticed she let the reference to his father slide. Everyone must know about his father's deterioration. Everyone but him.

"Honey Creek has nothing to hold me. You know what? You're the only person in Honey Creek other than my family who ever bothered to try to make contact with me in prison, the only one who wrote me. I never thanked you for that. I'm doing it now. Thank you."

As though she wasn't sure how to respond, she simply nodded.

"About that letter…" Dragging his hand through his longish hair, he grimaced. "I appreciate you writing it and I'm sorry I didn't answer."

"That was a long time ago. I probably shouldn't have written that."

"No." He laid his hand across the top of hers, unable to keep from noting the difference, his big and calloused while hers was slender, delicate and warm. "You probably shouldn't. But I was glad you did. You let me know that at least one person in Honey Creek believed in my innocence."

"If you felt that way, why didn't you write back?"

"Because your belief, my knowledge, was all futile. No matter what I knew, no matter what you thought, I'd been convicted. I was going to do time. Hard time. For Christ's sake, I was twenty when I went in there. I'm thirty-five now. I went in a kid and now…I'm a man. That does things to you. Prison does things to you." He hardened his voice. "I don't expect you to understand."

Pity flooded her eyes. He hated that and would have

gotten up and left if he hadn't seen something more there too, something besides pity.

"I'm so sorry," she said.

"Yeah. Me, too." Then, maybe because some demon drove him, he did what he'd been wanting to do since he'd seen her. He got up, crossed over to her side of the booth and kissed her.

Chapter 2

When Damien came around to her side of the booth and leaned over her, Eve's heart skipped a beat. As he bent close, she froze, feeling the way she imagined a deer in the headlights of a hunter's truck might feel.

And when his lips slanted over hers...she melted.

For a second, she allowed herself to revel in the feel of him, the taste and wonderful masculine scent of him, before gently pushing him away.

"Don't do that," she said, her voice shaky.

Damien leaned back, but didn't move away. Dark eyes glittering, he gave her a slow smile. "Why not?"

"Because I can't get involved with you."

"But you want to." Again he moved closer, making her pulse kick up once more.

"Yes," she admitted, licking her lips. "But I can't get involved with you or anyone right now. In any way, shape or form."

Just like that, his expression shut down. Moving stiffly, he pushed himself to his feet. "I understand."

He thought she was refusing him because he'd been in prison.

"No, you don't. Believe me."

"Whatever." Draining the last of his beer, he set the mug back on the table with a thud. "I'll go take care of the bill. You have a nice night, Eve."

Watching him walk away, she knew she should just let him go. "Wait," she called, causing both the bartender and Damien to look at her.

She shot the bartender a glare that had him turning away, suddenly busy with rearranging something behind the bar. Since Damien made no move to come back to her, she rose and walked to him instead. "If you'd just let me explain—"

"You don't have to." He cut her off, flashing her a twisted smile. Cramming his cowboy hat back on his head, he grabbed his coat from the coatrack and headed out the door.

Inexplicably close to tears, Eve watched him go. Then, avoiding the bartender's gaze, she grabbed her coat from the booth and made her way outside into the swirling, blowing snow.

Outside, the snowstorm seemed to be gathering strength. She hurried to her vehicle, shivering against the blustering wind.

Her Ford Explorer was old, but she kept it well-maintained. There was no reason for it not to start, but when she turned the key in the ignition and got only a quiet click, she knew she was in trouble.

Just to be sure, she tried again.

Nothing.

Breath blowing plumes in the frozen air, she checked

her watch. Ten o'clock. Nothing to do but go back inside the Corner Bar and see if the bartender would give her a ride home.

It was either that or call someone to come get her, and then she'd have to explain why she'd been at the bar drinking by herself.

Cursing under her breath, she pushed open the car door. The icy wind hit her like a slap to the face, making her raise the hood on her jacket as a shield. Hunched against the cold, she made her way back in the direction she'd come.

"Car trouble?" Damien Colton appeared out of the darkness, snow dusting his hair and shoulders.

Miserable, she nodded. "It won't start."

"Mind if I take a look?"

She handed over the car keys, watching as he attempted to start her car with the same results. "It's either your battery or the alternator. Either way, it's too cold and stormy to do anything about it tonight. I'll give you a ride home and you can deal with your car later."

"Great." She followed him to his pickup. At least now, he'd have no choice but to listen to her explanation.

The first thing she realized when she saw his truck was that it looked awfully familiar. "Is this the same—?"

"Truck I had back before I got convicted? Yes." He unlocked the passenger-side door and opened it for her, waiting while she climbed up before closing it.

The cab of the older truck had a bench seat. Thoughts of what she and Damien had once done on that very same seat made her flush warmly.

Once he'd gotten in, she watched as he started the engine, waiting for him to elaborate.

When he didn't, she sighed. "Look, about what I said earlier—"

"No need to explain." He cut her off brusquely. "You of all people don't owe me anything."

"I owe you an explanation. I don't want you thinking the reason I—"

Muttering a curse, he slammed on the brakes, sending the pickup into a spin on the snowy roads. They did a nearly perfect donut, ending up facing the same way they'd been going. Damien inched them forward, until they were on what appeared to be the shoulder of the road.

Then, while she still reeled with shock, he reached for her, yanking her up against him and capturing her mouth. He kissed her long and hard and deep. When he raised his head, Eve couldn't find her breath.

"What was that?"

"Me proving to you that you want me."

"I never said I didn't." She bit the inside of her cheek to keep from smiling. "I said I couldn't be in any sort of relationship with anyone right now."

"Relationship? Hell, I don't want a relationship."

Confused, she looked at him, so brooding and dark and dangerous. "Then what do you want?"

"Sex," he said, his tone harsh. "I just wanted to have sex with you."

Stunned, she couldn't think, couldn't speak, couldn't move. "Sex?" she finally repeated. "Wow, you certainly don't believe in sugarcoating it."

"Why call a spade anything other than a spade? I want you, Eve. You want me, too, I can tell. Neither one of us is attached right now and we're both adults. Why not?"

For a second she closed her eyes, tempted beyond belief. Massimo in Italy had wanted the same thing, just sex, though he'd prettied it up with honeyed words and candy-coated lies. In the end, she thought, it might have been better, at least for her, if he'd told the truth. Then maybe she wouldn't have felt like such a fool when it ended the way it had.

"I appreciate your honesty," she said slowly. "And yes, I do find you attractive. Very much so."

He crossed his arms, watching her, waiting. She recognized the look she saw on his face. He was expecting to be hurt, wounded, as he'd been for the last fifteen years. He really didn't believe she'd sleep with him, and any explanation she'd give him would reinforce his apparently deep-seated belief that he deserved to be treated poorly.

Any explanation that is, but the truth.

"Damien, I'm pregnant."

This he hadn't expected. "You're...what?"

"This summer I went to Italy. I took the trip by myself, to celebrate the last year of my thirties. When I was there, I met a man. We had the kind of thing you just proposed, only I didn't know it at the time." To her chagrin, her throat closed up.

"You're pregnant," he repeated.

"I'm pregnant."

"Does the father know?"

Now she hung her head. "This is the hardest part of my story. He disappeared. I looked for ten days, but I couldn't find him."

"You didn't know his name."

"He called himself Massimo. One word. Silly, but I thought it romantic."

Damien let that one go, bless him. "Are you keeping the baby?"

"Oh, yes." Cradling her stomach protectively, she nodded. "I want this baby very much. And you're the only one who knows."

Again she'd surprised him, judging from the look on his face. "You haven't told your family?"

"No. I'm waiting as long as I can." Oddly enough, telling him made her feel as though a heavy weight had been lifted from her shoulders. "You know how this town can be. My mom will be thrilled—she's been wanting a grandbaby for forever. But I feel sort of foolish, goofing up so badly at thirty-nine years old."

The truck heater started blasting, making them both laugh.

"I'd better get you home," he said, putting the truck back into gear.

He drove slowly, the heavy vehicle making sure progress over the snowy roads. When they reached her house, he left the engine running as he walked her to the door.

"If you ever need someone to talk to," he began, making her smile.

"Thank you. Ditto for you." Then, unable to help herself, she reached up and kissed him on the cheek.

Unmoving, he watched until she opened the door and went inside, locking it behind her.

A moment later she heard his truck drive away outside. Eyes stinging with completely unreasonable tears, she listened as the sound faded, until all she could hear was the mournful howling of the wind as it heralded the approaching storm.

Arriving back at the ranch, Damien breathed a sigh of relief when he saw that most of the cars were gone, which meant most of the huge mess of family had gone home. Except for the resident ones.

Parking his truck, he puzzled over Eve Kelley. Of all the girls he'd grown up with, he would have expected her to be married with a bunch of kids by now. Large families were common around these parts—look at his own family. She'd been pretty, popular and fun. The guys had practically fought over the chance to date her back in the day, and now she was nearly forty, unmarried and pregnant.

Talk about the randomness of fate.

None of it, not circumstances or her pregnancy, did anything to dilute his desire. He still wanted her. He'd take her up on her offer to be friends, knowing if she'd give him a chance, he'd prove to her that they could be more. Friends with benefits. He grinned savagely, liking the sound of that.

The house felt settled as he walked in, shedding his coat and hanging it in the hall closet and placing his cowboy hat on the hat rack alongside all the others. Lights from the immense Christmas tree illuminated the great room. All of the earlier boxes and mess had been cleaned away and the decorated mantel combined with the tree to look festive and, oddly enough, holy. Damien couldn't help but remember the way he'd felt as a small boy, awestruck and overwhelmed at the beautiful tree. He'd used to lie on his back underneath the branches and peer up through them, marveling.

To his surprise, a spark of that little boy still remained.

He wandered over and stood in front of the tree, still thinking of Eve, then eyed the hallway that led to his father's office. Might as well do some poking around while the entire house slept. Darius never locked the door, believing his inviolable authority made him invulnerable.

Maybe so, but Damien had been screwed over enough.

Moving quietly, he slipped down the hallway and opened the door. Conveniently, Darius had left the desk lamp on.

Damien took a seat in the massive leather chair and started with the obvious—the desk drawers. A quick search turned up exactly nothing.

But, then, what had he expected? Darius was too shrewd

to leave incriminating documents anywhere they could be easily read.

Which meant there had to be a safe.

He turned to begin searching for one when a movement from a shadowy corner made him spin around.

Duke stood watching him, leaning against the wall with his arms crossed.

"What are you doing?" Duke asked, "You know the old man's going to be pissed when he finds out you went through his papers."

"Maybe," Damien allowed. "*If* he finds out. I'm not planning on telling him. I'm trying to figure out what happened to our inheritance."

"What do you mean?"

Since Duke didn't sound too perturbed, Damien figured his brother hadn't been given the same unlikely story as he'd heard today. "I asked Darius about it earlier today. You know how I've been wanting to buy my own ranch, maybe in Nevada or Idaho?"

"Yeah." Duke uncrossed his arms and came closer. "Don't tell me he refused to give you your money. He might be conservator, but you're well over the age of twenty-one. And you were in prison at the time you turned twenty-one."

"No." Damien watched his brother closely. "He didn't refuse to give it to me. He said it was all gone."

"What?" Duke's casual air vanished. Shock filled his brown eyes, so like Damien's. "How can three million be gone, just like that?"

"Exactly. Tell me, bro. Did you get your inheritance when you turned twenty-one like you were supposed to?"

"Hell, no. He offered to let me use it to buy a share in the ranch and I took it. Darius needed cash for some reason, and I wanted to make sure I'd always have my house and land. So I bought my hundred acres from him."

"Damn." Damien closed his eyes. When he reopened them, he saw his brother watching him, a worried expression on his handsome face.

"Are you okay?"

"No," Damien exploded. "I'm not okay. The entire time I was in prison, I was counting on this money being there for me when I got out. The money the state's going to pay me won't buy even twenty acres. How the hell am I going to make a fresh start without any cash?"

"Surely there's been a mistake."

"I don't think so." Grimly, Damien resumed his search for a safe. "How good are you still at guessing lock combinations?"

"What? You mean to break into Darius's safe?"

"Once I find it, yes."

Duke narrowed his eyes. "Well, then, let me help you out. I know where it is. I've been in here often enough when Darius had to open it." He crossed to the wall where a huge, ornately framed oil painting of the ranch hung. "It's behind this."

Removing the picture revealed a small wall safe, black, with a touch-pad combination. The entire thing was maybe two feet square.

Damien stood back. "Have at it, bro." As teens, Duke had exhibited an exceptional skill for picking locks and determining combinations. Within five minutes, he had the safe open.

"There you go," he said, stepping back.

Reaching inside, Damien extracted a leather-bound notebook and a sheaf of manila folders, held together by a rubber band. There was also a tiny metal box, like the kind used for petty cash. He removed everything and placed it on the desk.

"I'm out of here, man," Duke said.

"Will you just stand guard for me? I just need a few minutes." He started with the leather book. "Surely there's something in here that will tell what happened to my inheritance."

Inside the book were receipts for wire transfers. All of them were withdrawals from his account made over a period of three years. "Bingo," he said softly. "My money."

Though clearly reluctant, Duke moved over to take a look.

"How do you know it was yours?" Duke asked. "You know when Grandfather died he left all of our money in the same account. I authorized Darius to take mine, and maybe Wes, Finn, Maisie and the others did the same."

"But I didn't authorize anything. Yet Darius claims the account has been closed and there's nothing there."

"Did you see the bank statement?"

"He wouldn't let me." Damien flashed him a grim smile, reaching for the manila folders. "Oh, damn."

"That looks like a second set of accounting records for the Colton ranch." Duke scratched his head. "Why would he have that? Unless..."

Without answering, Damien continued digging. "Look here. A list of some sort of vendors and receipts for transactions."

"Transactions of what?"

"I don't know." But he had a good idea. The FBI had approached him shortly after he'd been released from prison, intimating they were investigating Darius. Damien, still smarting from his father's refusal even to visit him in prison, had agreed to act as their insider, an informant of sorts. This was exactly the sort of thing they'd expect him to report.

"I think our father has been running a little business on the side."

Duke cursed. "What are you going to do? You can't be thinking of turning him in?"

"I don't know."

"Damien, you know how the old man is. I doubt he'd survive a year being locked up. I'm not sure I could do that to him."

"But then again, he didn't steal your money, did he? You handed it over to him, lock, stock and barrel."

"Please, think about this before you do anything rash."

Flipping through the last of the folders, Damien reached for the metal box. Duke reached for his hand to stop him. "Hold up."

"What?"

"You've found enough. Put it back. I think we need to talk to Wes and Finn before we do anything."

Clenching his jaw, Damien stared at his twin. "I'm not asking you to do anything."

"This is a family matter." Moving with purpose, Duke took the metal box, folder and notebook and placed them back in the safe, exactly the way they'd been. "We—or you—aren't doing anything until we talk to the others."

"What about Maisie?" Damien asked. "She has a right to be involved, too."

Duke shot him a hard glance. "If you can trust her to keep her mouth shut, fine. But you know, she's been contacting that TV show, trying to get them out here to do an exposé on the town."

"She's been talking about that, but I don't think anyone there took her seriously."

"I know. Let's keep it that way, okay?"

Reluctantly, Damien agreed, watching as Duke resecured the safe and replaced the painting.

"Come on," his brother said, putting a hand on Damien's shoulder. "Let's go to the kitchen and see if we can rustle up a late-night snack. There are bound to be some of those hot wings left."

Feeling both disgruntled and slightly relieved, Damien agreed. A decision needed to be made about Darius, but he wouldn't have to make it alone.

The next morning the snowplows worked the roads bright and early. Eve woke to the peculiar blinding whiteness of sun on snow. As she padded to the kitchen to make a pot of decaf and get the hearth fire going before letting Max out, she couldn't stop thinking of Damien and his offer.

Just looking at the man made her mouth go dry. What he proposed was very, very tempting. The fact that she could even think like this should have made her angry with herself, but she was pragmatic at heart and believed in calling a spade a spade.

Damien Colton made her go weak in the knees. Always had, always would.

The knowledge unsettled her. So much so that after she'd finished her first cup of coffee, she started cleaning her kitchen. She knew she'd find comfort in the physical work and satisfaction in the finished results.

About ninety minutes into her cleaning binge, when she'd finished the kitchen and the two bathrooms and started on the den, Max's barking alerted her that a car had pulled up into the drive. Her mother. Perspiring and grungy, and knowing she could use a break, Eve went to the front door and opened it wide.

"You're out bright and early on a snowy morning," she said brightly.

Bonnie Gene's gaze swept over her daughter. "It's not morning. It's well after noon."

"Well, good afternoon then." Eve wiped her hands on her sweats. "You caught me in the middle of cleaning. What's going on?" Moving aside, she waited until her mother entered before closing the door.

"I have fantastic news!" Bonnie Gene gushed the moment she stepped inside. Sweeping into the foyer in her usual dramatic fashion, she eyed Eve's pitiful attempts at Christmas decorating before focusing back on her daughter.

"You are not going to believe this. Guess what I've arranged?"

"I'm almost afraid to ask."

"Can the sarcasm." Too excited to note—or care about—Eve's less-than-enthusiastic reaction, Bonnie Gene clapped her gloved hands together. "I've set you up on a blind date."

"Not another blind date," Eve protested.

"This is not an ordinary blind date—it's the coup de grâce of all blind dates! You are going out with Gary Jackson!"

"Who?"

"You know, Gary Jackson the attorney? He just moved here a few months ago and I know for a fact all the single girls want to go out with him. He's tall, handsome and—"

"Full of himself." Eve dragged her hand through her hair. "Mother, we agreed. No more blind dates."

"*You* agreed. I said nothing. And listen, this one is too good to be true. You can't pass this up."

"Does he even know?"

Bonnie blinked. "What?"

"Does this Gary Jackson even know he has a blind date

with me? Remember, the last guy you set me up with and forced me to go on a date with had no idea. I was never so embarrassed in my life."

"Oh, for Pete's sake." Bonnie Gene rolled her eyes. "It all worked out, if I remember correctly."

"No, it didn't. He was a stalker, mother. I had to get Wes Colton involved. Thank goodness that guy left town."

Removing her coat, Bonnie Gene wandered into the great room, standing in front of the fire. "Ahhh. That feels so good. Listen, both Gary's mother and I went through a lot of work to arrange this. I'd really appreciate you going on this date. As a favor to me."

The old guilt trick. Eve refused to fall for it. "No."

"Come on. What else do you have to do?"

Eve crossed her arms. "Do you really want a list?"

Dropping down onto the couch, her mother sighed, removing her gloves and scarf and loosening her coat. "You know I only want what's best for you."

"Yes, but you've got to stop this obsessive trolling to find me a husband. I'm nearly forty. I can find my own man."

"Oh, can you?" Bonnie Gene pounced. "Then tell me, what have you been doing to try and meet someone?"

"Here we go again. Mother, don't start."

"Fine. But you know I want grandchildren."

If ever Eve had been tempted to reveal her pregnancy, now would be the time. But her mother would broadcast the news all over town and right now, with the Mark Walsh fiasco in full swing, the last thing Honey Creek needed was more scandal. Nope, Eve just wanted to get through the holidays before dropping her bombshell.

"I know you want grandchildren, Mother. You've informed me of that nonstop for the last ten years."

"Well, then," Bonnie said brightly. "Since I've already arranged this date, will you please go?"

Bonnie Gene looked so contrite, Eve softened. As she always did. Sucker. "I'll go, but only if you give me your absolute word that this is the last blind date you arrange for me."

Grinning, Bonnie Gene nodded. "Do you want me to pinky swear?"

"Just give me your word, Mother."

"Fine." Huffing, Bonnie Gene grimaced. "You have my word. No more blind dates."

"Ever."

"Fine. No more blind dates ever." Her frown faded and she grinned. "Maybe this date with Gary Jackson will lead to something permanent and you won't *need* another blind date."

Oh geez. "Maybe. Who knows?" Sighing, Eve went into the kitchen. "Would you like a cup of tea?"

"I'd love one. Do you want my help picking out an outfit for your date?"

Midway to the kitchen, Eve paused. Turning, she eyed her mother, dreading the answer yet knowing she had to ask.

"When is this date with Gary Jackson, by the way?"

"Tonight."

Chapter 3

Eve nearly said a curse word in front of her mother. "Tonight? How could you do this to me?"

"Please," Bonnie scoffed. "You've got over six hours to get ready. It's not like you have to be there for lunch or anything."

"Where's there?"

"You're meeting him for drinks and dinner at the Corner Bar and Grill."

Of course. Her mother knew that was Eve's favorite place, as well as the second-most popular place in town, Kelley's Cookhouse being first.

Putting the kettle on the stove, Eve got out two mugs and two teabags of orange pekoe tea.

"Everyone will see me there," she groused, secretly glad her mother hadn't chosen to have her meet Gary at the family's barbecue restaurant. She'd done that before and Eve had spent the entire evening answering questions about what it was like to be part of the family that owned a famous franchised restaurant. Worse, her date had expected free food and had ordered one of everything on the menu. He'd been shocked, then angry, when Eve had informed him they still had to pay.

"Exactly! There's a live band tonight, the High Rollers, I think. So you know the place will be packed. Everyone will see you there with Gary," Bonnie enthused. "That man is quite a catch. The town will be talking about it for days!"

A catch? Mentally, she rolled her eyes. "Honestly, Mom. I'm not exactly fishing."

"No, you're not," her mother said with a wry twist of her mouth. "Which is why I have to help you. You've got me baiting the hook and casting for you. Now all you've got to do is reel him in."

Reel him in. Had they been mysteriously teleported back to the fifties when she hadn't been looking? Deciding to ignore the phrase, as she always did when Bonnie Gene started on this subject, Eve stared at the teakettle, willing it to whistle. A good cup of tea went far to sooth frazzled nerves.

Taking her silence for assent, Bonnie Gene came closer. "What are you going to wear? If you'd like, I could pick out your outfit."

"Oh, for—" Biting off the words, Eve forced a smile. "Mom, don't worry about that. I've got it covered."

Six hours later, standing in front of the mirror, Eve wondered why she'd agreed to this. She couldn't help but wonder if Gary Jackson wondered the same thing. If he was such a "catch," as her mother put it, she doubted he needed to be set up on a blind date.

But, heavens knows, Bonnie Gene Kelley could be pretty persistent when she wanted to be.

For her dinner date, Eve had chosen a thick sweaterdress with a cowl neckline in flattering shades of brown, cream and gold. Brown leggings and soft suede knee-length boots completed her outfit. She brushed her shoulder-length blond hair until it shone, swiped a tube of lip gloss over her lips, and told herself she was ready.

In fact, she'd rather be doing almost anything else. Even pooper-scooping Max's poo seemed preferable to yet another blind date set up by her own mother. How pathetic was that?

Still, she reminded herself, slipping on her parka and snagging her purse and car keys on her way out, none of this was Gary Jackson's fault. He could be a nice guy. She should give him a chance.

Thirty minutes later, covertly checking her watch, she knew she'd been wrong. From the instant she'd walked into the Corner Bar and taken a seat in the booth across from him, Gary Jackson had talked nonstop. About his law practice, what kind of car he drove, what stocks he'd invested in, where he lived and what kind of furniture graced his abode, blah, blah, blah. Every single time she thought he might be winding down, he'd start on another tangent. About himself, of course.

No wonder the guy couldn't find a date. She'd be willing to bet he'd jumped on the chance when her mother had offered her as the sacrificial lamb.

Poker-faced, she sipped her soft drink and tried to keep from yawning. Even on a weekend date, the man wore a button-up shirt and tie, along with a wool sport jacket and slacks.

"Anyway, when they asked me to help out with the Mark Walsh investigation..."

Finally, something interesting. "You're helping out with that? How? You're a lawyer, not a criminal investigator."

She'd barely got the words out before Gary was off and running. Not about the Mark Walsh case, which she might have been interested in hearing, instead, he rambled on about how anyone, even the lowliest criminal, needed an attorney and how lucky the people of backwater Honey Creek, Montana, were to have him. Because he was the best, the brightest, the most like a shark, etc.

While she sat, steaming and wishing she could drink alcohol. Since she couldn't, she practiced scathing remarks she'd like to say but couldn't.

Finally, she'd had enough. "Excuse me," she tried to interrupt. Either Gary had gone hard of hearing or was so involved in what he was saying that she had to repeat herself three times. In the end, she simply got to her feet, waved her hand at him, and headed toward the restroom. She could have sworn he continued talking to the air after she'd left.

This was a disaster. If it weren't that her mother would find out, she'd sneak out the back and leave him talking to himself.

The hallway to the restrooms was long and blessedly deserted. She took her time, aware that every second away from Gary was a second of peace and quiet. Finally she had no choice but to make her way back.

"Eve?" a deep familiar voice called her name.

Looking up, her heart skipped a beat. Her body, numbed by Gary's endless rambling, came gloriously, fully awake and alive. "Damien." She tried to sound casual. "What are you doing here?"

"Hoping to run into you," he answered, making her blush. "And here you are." He sounded so pleased, she had to smile. "Do you want to join me for a drink and a snack? Just to talk."

Talk about tempting. She had a brilliant idea. "I can't

join you, because I'm here with someone." Quickly she told him about her mother's scheme and Gary Jackson. "I want out of this, but I can't get him to shut up long enough to tell him so. Please, join us for dinner. Maybe then he'll get the hint."

Expression serious, he studied her face. "This is the second time I've helped you out, you know. After this, you'll owe me a date, just the two of us."

"Done." She'd have agreed to almost anything to end the torture of Gary, but a date with Damien seemed more like a reward than a payment of a debt. "So that means you'll help me out? I hate to ask, but…"

His smile took her breath away. "Sure, I will. But first, come here."

Pulse kicking back up, she didn't move. "No."

"Chicken."

"Maybe," she acknowledged. "But I need to know what you mean."

"A simple kiss. That's all I want."

"Here?"

He glanced around. "Sure, why not? We're in a dark hallway and unless someone comes down this way, no one will see."

Temptation. She realized suddenly that there was nothing she wanted more than to kiss him. But not the kind of kiss she could do here, standing in a hallway in the Corner Bar.

"My kiss," he reminded her. "Yes or no? Your call."

Moving closer, but standing far enough back that no part of their bodies touched, she leaned in, intent on making this a quick, touch-her-lips-to-his, peck-type kiss.

Instead, he yanked her up to him. "Real kiss," he growled. "I haven't been able to stop thinking about our last one. Now lay it on me."

At first she couldn't move. Paralyzed by indecision and the knowledge that the blind date from hell waited in the other room, she let panic immobilize her. For maybe all of three seconds.

Then she reached up and pulled him down to her. Slanting her mouth over his, she kissed him like they were alone in her bedroom, kissed him like she'd secretly been longing to do ever since she'd seen him, kissed him openmouthed and insistent and full of pent-up longing and desire.

When she finally raised her head, they were both breathing hard.

"There," she said, trying for a light teasing tone. "Now will you join me for dinner?"

Eyes dark and glittering, he nodded.

"Come on then." She took his arm. "Let me introduce you two. My date thinks he's an expert on the Mark Walsh investigation, though for the life of me I don't know what he has to do with it."

From the sudden tension in Damien's body, she judged she'd said the wrong thing. But there was no time to fix it since they'd almost reached the table.

Gary stood, appearing comically surprised that she'd already returned. Or, she surmised, watching his eyes widen as he saw Damien, shocked that she'd brought back an escort, especially one as big and muscular and male as Damien.

Speaking briskly, she made the introductions. "Gary Jackson, Damien Colton. Damien, Gary."

The two men shook hands. Then Damien pulled out a chair and, instead of taking a seat, turned it around and straddled it. "Let me buy you both a drink. What are you drinking, Gary?"

"Scotch on the rocks, neat," Gary responded. Since Eve

knew he'd been drinking a beer, she shot him a look, which he promptly ignored.

Trying not to watch Damien, trying not to think about that kiss and what else she wanted to do with him, she watched Gary instead. For once, eying Damien, her formerly talkative date appeared at a loss for words.

Signaling the waitress, Damien ordered. "Scotch for him, Coors Light for me, and a Shirley Temple for the lady."

"How'd you know that's what she was drinking?" Gary asked.

Damien shrugged. "Eve and I go way back. She was telling me you're involved in the Mark Walsh murder investigation? How so?"

"Part of my job dictates that I occasionally have to do pro bono work as a public defender. When—and if—the police find any suspects, I'm on call in case they can't afford an attorney." He spread his hands. "They won't even realize how lucky they are. I was the best criminal attorney in Fargo before I moved here and switched to private practice."

Eve glared at him. "So you're actually not working on the case then. You're just prepared to help if they need you?"

Before he could answer, Damien stood, waving. "Maisie. Over here."

Wearing a full-length fake fur and stiletto-heeled boots, Maisie Colton looked like a glamorous movie star. She breezed up to their table, giving Damien a quick hug before turning to face Eve and Gary.

"Hi, Eve," she said dismissively, turning to Gary, eyeing his clean-cut features and business attire. "Who are you? I don't believe we've met."

"Maisie Colton, meet Gary Jackson. Gary, this is Maisie, Damien's sister."

To Eve's amazement, Gary's face turned beet-red as he took Maisie's perfectly manicured hand. "My pleasure," he murmured, kissing her hand.

It took every bit of Eve's self-restraint to keep from rolling her eyes. She didn't dare glance at Damien to see his reaction.

For her part, Maisie appeared to be eating it up. Fluttering her long lashes, she took a seat, perching on the end of the bench. "I can't believe I haven't met you. Have you been in town long?"

Gary had to lean across the table to hear her breathy question, jabbing Eve with his elbow in the process.

"You know what?" Eve said, pushing to her feet. "I think I'm going to have to call it a night. It was nice to meet you, Gary."

"Likewise," he said, never tearing his gaze away from Maisie's perfect features. "Have a nice night."

"Excuse me." Damien nudged Maisie to get up so he could get out. "I need to be going, too."

Maisie slid out without protest, taking her seat back immediately after Damien stood. As Eve turned to go she saw Maisie reach across the table and capture Gary's hand.

"They deserve each other," Damien said, helping Eve on with her coat. "Let me walk you to your truck."

"This will be all over town by morning." Glancing around, Eve saw half of the place watching her and Damien and the other half staring at Gary and Maisie.

"Gossip. Don't worry about it."

"Easy for you to say. You forget, I run a beauty shop, aka gossip central. I will hear about this on Tuesday, both from my customers and from my mother." She brightened.

"Though at least I can blame Maisie for the failed date. That way I don't have to tell my mother that I thought Gary was a jerk."

One hand on the door handle, Damien stopped and studied Eve's face. "You seem to spend a lot of time pretending to be something you're not. That's not the Eve Kelley I remember."

Stunned, she could only retort with the first thing that came to her. "Maybe your memory's faulty."

Brushing past him, she slipped out the door.

She should have known he wouldn't give up that easily.

"Eve, wait."

"Oh, won't this give them something to talk about," she groused.

"Why are you so worried about what people think?"

"I'm not." With a sigh, she acknowledged her lie. "Okay, maybe I am. A little. But you have to understand what will happen when I open the salon tomorrow. Every one of my customers, whether or not they have an appointment, will be stopping by to ask about this."

"Are you sure you're not exaggerating?"

Tilting her head, she thought for a second. "I'm sure."

"What about him?" He jerked his head toward the bar. "Is he all right to leave with Maisie?"

"Oh, sure." Unable to suppress a grin, she shook her head. "Who knows? Maybe they're perfect for each other."

"Maybe. Eve, I—"

Suddenly skittish, Eve took a step back. "Damien, I've got to go."

One corner of his mouth lifted in an amused smile. "Have a nice night. I'll see you tomorrow then."

This stopped her short. "Tomorrow? For what?"

"Our date. Remember?"

Her stomach rolled. "You didn't say it would be so soon."

He took a step toward her, causing her to move back. "Eve, what are you so afraid of? Is it me?"

Oh, God, did he really think she was like some of the other people in town, frightened of him because he'd been in prison?

"It's not that. I told you, I don't want or need to get involved with anyone right now."

"We don't have to get involved." He held out his hand. "Just friends."

Blood humming, she stared at him. Then, slowly, she took his hand. "Friends," she said. Because the feel of his large, calloused hand enveloping hers made her want to touch more of him, she jerked her hand free. Moving so quickly she slid on the snow-covered ice, she headed for her car with the sound of his very male laughter following her.

Watching Eve drive away, Damien debated returning to the Corner Bar and finishing his beer. Finally, he decided against it, not wanting to interfere with Maisie and her apparent fascination with Eve's blind date. Still, he had to see if his sister wanted a ride home.

Entering the bar's warmth, he headed for the booth. Maisie and Gary were so engrossed in conversation that neither noticed his approach.

"Maisie, I'm about to head home."

"Oh." She pouted, slanting a look of invitation at Gary under her long eyelashes. "Then I guess I have to go."

"I can drive you home later," Gary gallantly offered.

In response, her brilliant smile was designed to blind. Tongue in cheek, Damien watched as the other man fell for it, hook, line and sinker. Poor guy could barely form a coherent thought, he was so taken with Maisie.

Kind of the way Damien felt about Eve.

Saying his goodbyes, Damien headed back into the cold and climbed into his pickup.

On the way home, acting completely on impulse, he turned down the road that led toward Eve's place. Yellow light beamed from the windows, warm and inviting. Cruising to a stop in front of her house, he eyed the beautiful log home. What would she do if he went up and rang the doorbell? Would she let him in or turn him away?

Debating, he finally put the truck in Drive and turned around, this time heading back to the Colton ranch.

Arriving at home, he parked and went around to the back door, knowing this way he had a better chance of avoiding Darius if he were skulking around and drinking. Coming in through the mudroom, off the back downstairs bathroom, he opened the door quietly, trying to make as little noise as possible, and just about ran into Jeremy, Maisie's fourteen-year-old son.

Even with the lights off, Damien could see the boy had been crying. Tears still glittered on his adolescent cheeks.

"Are you okay?" Damien asked, hating the inane question, but not sure if his nephew would welcome his intrusion.

"No." Jeremy sniffed, swiping at his face. "I'm not okay."

Which meant either Darius or Maisie had done something. And, since Maisie was still in town with Gary Jackson, his money was on Darius.

"What's the matter?"

"Darius," Jeremy snarled. "Darius is what's the matter."

The first time Damien had heard his nephew address

his grandfather by his given name, he'd been startled, but Maisie had told him Darius had forbidden the use of any name relating to grandfather. Figured. He'd always refused to allow his own children to call him Dad or even Father.

"What about Darius?" Damien asked cautiously. "What's he done now?"

"What hasn't he done? He makes my mother look like a saint. He's crazy."

Instantly wary, since he'd thought pretty much the same thing, Damien scratched his head. "Maybe so," he allowed. "But you still haven't told me what happened."

About to speak, Jeremy made a gagging sound and jerked away. He ran for the toilet and hunched over it while he threw up.

Alcohol? Food poisoning? Damien tried to remember all the crazy stunts he himself had tried at fourteen. He'd only been home a few months, but from what he'd seen of Jeremy, the kid appeared to be a real straight arrow.

Waiting patiently, Damien handed his nephew a paper towel to wipe his mouth.

"You've got to help me," the boy blurted. "Darius said he's selling my horse."

"What?" Damien drew back. "Why? What'd you do?"

Selling someone's horse was the worst possible punishment for a cowboy on a ranch. A horrible suspicion occurred to him. "Were you drinking or using drugs?"

"No." Now Jeremy appeared shocked. "Of course not. Darius caught me smoking cigarettes out by the barn."

Cigarettes? "When did you start smoking?"

"I didn't. I just wanted to try them to see what they were like."

"Ah, I see. I'm guessing he took them away?"

"No." The teenager gagged again, staggering back to the commode and retching. This started him crying again.

Through his sobs, he glared up at Damien. "Darius made me eat them."

"Eat them? I don't understand."

"He fed me the cigarettes. One by one. Made me chew and swallow each and every one of them, even the one I'd started to smoke." The kid started looking green again. He swallowed hard. "And now I'm sick."

Stunned, Damien couldn't understand his father's logic. "That's..."

"Crazy. I know, right?"

"Yeah." Damien, too, had tried cigarettes around that age. He hadn't liked it, and had never picked up a pack again, even in prison, where there were so little pleasures that men took whatever they could get.

He waited until Jeremy seemed all right.

"How long ago did this happen?"

"Half an hour. Why?"

"Just wondering where Darius is."

Anger flashed again in the teenager's eyes. "I don't know."

"Where's everyone else?"

Lifting one thin shoulder in a shrug, Jeremy gagged again. "Dunno."

Which meant no one else was around. Duke was probably out with Susan and Wes and Finn had long ago gone home. Damien and Maisie had both been in town.

Jeremy had been left on his own with Darius. Sure, Sharon had probably been here, but the woman stayed in her room ninety percent of the time.

Damn. Damien wanted to punch something. Or someone. He really didn't want another confrontation with Darius right now.

"If he sells Charger, I'm going to run away," Jeremy vowed. "I've raised that gelding from a colt."

"I know you have," Damien soothed. "I've heard he's a fine stock horse, too."

"He ought to be." Jeremy lifted his chin, furiously wiping at his tear-streaked cheeks. "I've spent the better part of three years working with him."

"That long?"

"Yep. Darius gave him to me for my eleventh birthday."

"That settles it. You can't take back a birthday present."

"I know. But you know what he said? If he gives, he can sure as hell take away."

"I'll talk to him," Damien heard himself promise. "I won't let him sell Charger."

Jeremy lifted his head. Hope flashed in his young face. "You mean it?" Then, before Damien could answer, the fourteen-year-old launched himself at his uncle, barreling into him and wrapping his arms around him tightly.

"I'll try," Damien choked out.

"Thank you, thank you," the boy muttered fervently. "I can't let anything happen to Charger. He's all I've got."

Something in the kid's broken tone reminded Damien of himself. Except Jeremy at least had a horse. Damien had nothing and no one. But then, he didn't need anyone. Jeremy plainly did.

"You have your mother," Damien pointed out. "She might have her problems, but she loves you."

"I guess."

Ruffling the kid's hair, Damien slung his arm across his shoulders. "No guessing about it. I know. Now come on. Let's see if I can rustle us up any of the mulled apple cider they were drinking the other day."

Jeremy nodded.

As they started walking toward the kitchen, they heard a scream. Loud, feminine and terrified.

"Wait here." Pushing the kid back, Damien rushed into the great room. There, cowering in a corner near the fireplace, crouched Sharon, Darius's wife. Darius stood over her holding a fire poker.

Chapter 4

"Darius." Damien spoke in a calm, measured voice. "What are you doing?"

When the older man swung his head around and attempted to focus his bloodshot eyes on his son, Damien realized his father was once again drunk.

Smashed, plastered, blotto.

Behind him, he heard a gasp. Jeremy had ignored his request to stay behind.

"Jeremy, go back in the kitchen."

"No." The fourteen-year-old's voice wavered, but he stood his ground.

Damien returned his attention to his father. "Put the poker down."

"This is a family matter," Darius snarled. "Nothing to do with you."

The inference being that he wasn't family. Used to his father's jabs, Damien ignored that, aware he had to steer

Darius away from Sharon. Redirecting his anger might be the only way to accomplish that. But first, he had to make sure Jeremy was out of the way.

"What are you doing, Darius?" Damien moved closer, praying his nephew had the good sense to stay back. "Sharon's your wife. Surely you don't mean to hurt her?"

Confusion briefly flashed across Darius's mottled face, before the alcohol-inspired rage replaced it. "She belongs to me, boy. I'll do whatever I damn well please."

Sharon made a soft moan of pain, drawing Darius's attention.

"Darius," Damien barked, taking another step forward. "Like hell you will. You'll have to go through me first."

"Fine," Darius snarled. "I will."

He swung the poker at Damien at the same moment as Damien kicked out his leg. The old man fell, the poker went flying into the bricks with a clatter, and Sharon Colton crumpled to the rug, unconscious.

Narrowly missing hitting his head on the hearth, Darius let out a bellow of fury and frustration and pain as he climbed toward his feet, starting for his wife.

After kicking the fireplace tool over to Jeremy, Damien grabbed his father, afraid Darius would start whaling on Sharon with his fists next.

Instead, as Damien wrapped him in a bear hug, the elder Colton folded up into himself, wrapping his arms around his own middle and rocking. Crying great sobs, he mumbled under his breath to himself, tears streaming down his face, all the while shooting an occasional death glare up at his son.

Not sure how to take this bizarre behavior, Damien glanced at Jeremy. The teen appeared flabbergasted and shell-shocked. Not good. He needed something to do.

"Jeremy, check on Sharon." Barking out the order, he saw his nephew jump. "Make sure she's breathing."

While Jeremy hurried over, Damien slowly let go of his father, who had hunched over and was now making a soft keening sound, like a wounded animal.

Obviously, he had more going on than a problem with alcohol.

"She's breathing," Jeremy said, checking his stepmother's pulse. "I think she just fainted."

"Okay, good." Trying to think what to do, Damien fished his cell phone out of his pocket and called his twin brother.

"Be right there," Duke said, after Damien explained the situation.

Darius's keening grew louder.

"What's wrong with him?" Wide-eyed, Jeremy stared at his grandfather. "Is he having a stroke?"

"I don't know. He's having something. Let's see if we can get Sharon to wake up. I want to make sure she didn't hit her head or injure herself in any way."

As soon as he got close to Sharon, Damien smelled the strong scent of alcohol. "She's been drinking," he said flatly.

"Maybe she and Darius were drinking together."

"Maybe." But in his experience, Darius's wife did as little as possible with her husband. In fact, she seemed to go out of her way to avoid him. His brothers had already begun taking bets as to how long she could hold out.

During his time home with Darius, Damien couldn't blame her. If he were in her shoes, he'd have hightailed it out of Honey Creek a long time ago.

Maybe she was like him. He took another look at her, still out of it and now snoring peacefully. Maybe she had nowhere else to go and no money of her own to make a new life. As with both his previous wives, Darius had most likely made her sign a prenup, ensuring she got nothing if she left.

"Hey, guys. What happened?" The tension seemed to dissipate slightly as Duke strode into the room. Ignoring their father, who'd gone silent and appeared to have passed out, he crossed to Damien and Jeremy.

Briefly, Damien relayed the night's events, letting Jeremy interject with his story. When they'd finished, Duke shook his head. "You know, Maisie's been trying to tell me things were getting bad here. I thought she was being her usual melodramatic self."

"If Maisie's been dealing with stuff like this, why the hell is she leaving Jeremy here alone?"

Duke looked directly at Jeremy. "Have you witnessed this sort of behavior much before now?"

"No, sir, not this bad. Lot's of yellin' and name-callin'. But nothing physical. Not like this at all. Darius hasn't ever acted so crazy."

"He's drunk," Damien said. "Not that being soused excused him acting like this, but it sure helps explain it."

"How do you know he's drunk?" Duke asked.

"Go take a whiff of him. He smells like he's taken a bath in Scotch."

"And Sharon's drunk, too," Jeremy added. "But she smells more like wine than hard stuff."

"I'll take your word for it. That's all the proof I need." Duke didn't even bother walking over to Darius. "Will you help me get Sharon to her room?"

"Sure," Damien nodded. "But what about him?"

"We'll come back and get him next."

Once they had both Darius and his wife safely in their separate beds, they all trooped in to the kitchen.

Rummaging in the refrigerator, Damien located the jug of apple cider and poured them each a glass.

"How long has this been going on?" Duke asked, dropping his large frame into a chair.

"You tell me." Crossing his arms, Damien faced his twin.

"Hey, I don't live here. You do. I knew his mental stability appeared to be shaky, but I had no idea he was this bad. I've never seen him like this. I don't want to ever see him like this again."

"He threatened to sell my horse," Jeremy put in. "And made me eat an entire pack of cigarettes."

"He did what?" Maisie, carrying her high heels and walking on stocking feet, entered the kitchen. "Where is that sorry sack of—"

"He's unconscious." Damien cut her off. "Passed out. He was stone-cold drunk when I got here."

"He attacked Sharon with the fire thingee," Jeremy put in. "We had to stop him from bashing her head in."

Maisie nodded, apparently unconcerned, then went to the cabinet, grabbed a glass and helped herself to some apple cider. "So where is he now?"

"Duke and I carried him to his room."

"I hope you left him on the floor. That would serve him right for what he did."

"Maise?" Damien leaned forward. "You're around here more than anyone. How long has he been this bad?"

Her angry smile faded. "A good while. But he seemed to get worse after you got out of prison."

"Has he attacked you?" Duke sounded horrified. And Damien noticed the way Jeremy suddenly seemed to find the kitchen floor absolutely fascinating.

"Nothing I couldn't handle," Maisie snapped. But her

heightened color told them all she was lying. Maisie always blushed when she wasn't telling the truth.

They all sat in silence for a moment, Damien trying to digest this sudden, radical shift in his world.

"You didn't know about this?" Duke directed his question at Damien.

"Hell, no. I spend as little time here at the house as possible. Most days I'm out riding herd on the cattle or checking the fences and pastures. What about you?"

"I don't live here. So no, I knew the old man seemed a little off, but not to this extent."

"He must have had an iron grip on his control all this time and now it's slipping. I've seen men like that in prison."

"We've got to do something," Duke mused. "But what?"

Maisie rolled her eyes. "As long as he doesn't hurt anybody..."

"He nearly hurt Sharon. And he made Jeremy eat an entire pack of cigarettes."

"True." She rounded on her son. "I want you to stay away from him, you hear me?"

Instantly defensive at her sharp tone, Jeremy's expression changed into that sullen, bored look all teenagers master. Damien remembered it well from his own childhood.

"I'd like to run away from here," Jeremy mumbled.

Perfect. "You know what?" Damien pushed to his feet. "Once I get the financial problem settled, I'm out of here. Maisie, Jeremy, you're both welcome to come with me."

"Awesome!"

"Financial problem?" Maisie frowned. "Just get your inheritance. That should be enough."

Damien exchanged a look with Duke. "Uh, yeah, about that. Maise, did you get your money?"

"No. Darius keeps it for me. He puts a monthly allowance

in my checking account so I can shop." She glanced from one to the other, narrowing her eyes. "Why?"

Damien told her about his conversation with Darius, finishing with, "I'm trying to find out exactly what happened to the money."

"Be careful," she said darkly. "I have a feeling there are things about Darius that we're all better off not knowing." She went to her son and put her arm around him, ignoring his sounds of protest.

"Come on, Jeremy. Time to go to bed. You've got school in the morning. As a matter of fact…" Her bright-aqua gaze pinned Damien and then Duke. "You two should turn in, too. Though the sun rises later this time of the year, you know how much work there will be in the morning."

She left, dragging Jeremy with her. After she'd gone, Damien glanced at Duke. "What do you know? Our big sister actually sounded practical."

"I know." Duke grabbed his Stetson and crammed it back on his head. "And she's right. I'm heading home. I'll see you tomorrow morning at the barn."

Locking the door behind him, Damien trudged up the stairs to his room, hoping the bone-deep exhaustion he felt would allow him finally to get a good night's sleep.

The next morning Damien woke pissed off and aroused. He needed a woman. Immediately, he thought of Eve. He'd been dreaming about her again. He couldn't help but hope that eventually, she might want him, too. Even if she had refused his offer to become his bedroom partner, he'd seen the desire in her beautiful blue eyes.

But for now, he'd leave her alone. As he'd done in the past, he'd find other outlets for his need. Meanwhile, he'd put in a call to his brother Wes, asking to meet him at the Corner Bar for lunch. He had several things he wanted to discuss with him, especially Darius's behavior.

Damien hurried through his morning preparations, showering and dressing in a hurry. On his way out, he stopped in the kitchen and picked up one of the sausage breakfast sandwiches the cook made for the ranch hands and a cup of hot coffee. Then he hurried outside, turning up the collar of his down jacket against the biting ice of the winter wind.

Walking to the barn, he finished the last bite of the sandwich, washing it down with the hot coffee. Fortified, he slipped on his gloves and went to saddle up his gelding. He'd ride out and join Duke and the other hands, aware they had to bring the cattle in from the pastures in the higher elevations before the forecasted blizzard.

They finished driving the cattle shortly before noon. Damien brushed down his horse and washed up in the barn washroom, before driving into town. He parallel-parked on Main Street and fed the meter, surprised that he'd managed to snag a primo parking spot, even if it was a block or two away from the Corner Bar. He didn't mind. Walking, especially in brisk, cold air like this, cleansed the spirit and cleared the mind.

Being in town wasn't so bad, he thought, feeling pretty upbeat for a change. Until he neared a group of Christmas shoppers and they crossed the street to avoid him.

Familiar anger filled him. Striding down Main Street, face lifted to the brisk December wind, he tried to pretend he didn't care, that he was just enjoying the invigorating winter day. It wasn't easy keeping his expression pleasant, trying not to notice how many people avoided his eyes, pretended not to see him or, worse, crossed to the other side of Main Street as the last group had, simply to avoid being in the same space as Damien Colton, ex-felon.

Going on four months out of prison and the citizens of Honey Creek, Montana, still treated him like a criminal.

Even though he'd known most of them all his life, to them he'd forever be branded Damien Colton, the murderer. It didn't matter to them that he'd been completely exonerated. Or that the body of the man he'd supposedly killed had turned up, really dead this time, fifteen years after his mockery of a trial. Now, even though the town was all abuzz while the authorities tried to find the real killer, all anyone around here saw when they looked at him was an ex-con.

He'd gone to prison a boy of twenty. Fifteen years later he'd emerged a man of thirty-five who might just as well have had a flashing scarlet letter—*K* for Killer—branded on his forehead.

Shrugging off the bitterness, he entered the Corner Bar, so different in the daytime, and looked around, helpless to keep from marking how many gazes slid past him the minute he looked their way. Every time he came to town, the reasons he needed to collect his inheritance and move far away became clearer and clearer.

His brother Wes waved him over from a booth in the back. Relieved to see at least one friendly face, Damien headed that way, head held high, shoulders back. In prison he'd learned many things, but the most important was the ability to present himself to others as full of self-confidence. It helped to behave as though his hometown's massive shunning of him didn't bother him at all.

His favorite bartender, a tattooed guy named Jack Huffman, who'd moved to Honey Creek from out of town and didn't care about any of the drama concerning Mark Walsh, the man Damien had supposedly murdered, saw him coming and met him at the table with a tall draft beer in a frosted mug.

"Ahhh." Sliding into the booth across from Wes, Damien took a long pull of the icy beer, reveling in the taste. Of all the things he'd missed while incarcerated, the taste of a good brew ranked right up there.

Both men ordered cheeseburgers, the Corner Bar's specialty, and another delicacy Damien had missed while locked up.

Would he ever stop thinking of things in that way? How everything related to the wasted years? As he did every day, he vowed to try. More than anything, he wanted to feel like a regular cattle rancher again. Unfortunately, he had begun to realize he'd have to leave Honey Creek to be able to do so.

"I haven't found out anything else about Mark Walsh's death," Wes said, assuming that's why Damien had asked to meet him. "The investigation is still ongoing. The FBI people have been a lot of help, but we still don't have anything new."

"I didn't think so." Absurdly uncomfortable, Damien dragged his hand through his longish brown hair, so different from Wes's closely shaven head, and sighed. Then he straightened his shoulders and transformed himself into the supremely self-confident, don't-mess-with-me Damien he embodied to confront difficult situations. "I need your help in another matter."

"Shoot. Does this have anything to do with you disappearing a couple of times a month?" Clearly intrigued, Wes leaned forward. "What's up?"

"I disappear every so often because I'm not a monk or a priest. Celibacy just isn't my thing," Damien drawled. "I went fifteen years without. After being locked up, I thought I was used to it, but I can't do it. So I drive up to Bozeman, sometimes Billings."

Wes sat back, shaking his head. "You haven't met anyone local yet?"

Trying not to think of Eve, Damien looked his brother

right in the eye. "You know as well as I do that every single woman in Honey Creek runs the other way when she sees me coming."

"Have you even tried?"

"Tried? Hell, I've spent so many nights sitting around this bar and a couple of others, that I've lost count. I can't even get a woman to dance with me, never mind take me home." Other than Eve Kelley, he thought silently. This was something he wanted to keep to himself for now.

"I think that might be your own fault." Now Wes pinned Damien with a stare. "I've heard you drink yourself blind, act surly and mean and scare away anyone—man or woman—from even talking to you."

Stung, Damien grimaced. "Where'd you hear that from? Your girlfriend?"

"Fiancée. And no, Lily hasn't been spying on you. A couple of my deputies have seen you."

Frustration nearly made Damien scowl. Instead, he used his poker face, knowing if he wanted Wes's help, he had to play nice. "Bottom line. When I need a woman, I head out of town. It's a long drive to Billings and I'm getting tired of it."

"Once or twice a month. Man." Wes whistled. "That's so—"

"I know. Cut the sympathy. You've got a woman."

Wes spread his hands. "What can I do?"

"Come on, you're in law enforcement. You've seen the seedier side of life. You know how back in high school there were girls who were…"

"Fast?"

"Exactly." He shifted his weight. "I've been away for fifteen years while you've been here. You know everyone. Surely you can point me in the right direction."

To Damien's chagrin and frustration, this time Wes laughed out loud.

"What's so funny?"

Wes stopped laughing long enough to answer. "You're really serious."

"Wouldn't you be, if our positions were reversed?"

"Maybe," Wes allowed.

"Maybe? Come on, tell the truth."

"Look." All trace of amusement vanished from Wes's face. "You just need to make friends with someone here in town. We've got plenty of single women. You could hook up with any one of them, if you'd just make the effort."

As if it was that simple. What Wes conveniently forgot to mention is that if any single woman in Honey Creek dated him, a Colton, she'd expect a lot more than a simple sexual relationship. Assuming she could look past the been-in-prison thing.

"I told you, I don't want anything complicated. I just want sex."

"Good luck with that."

"Then I guess I'll keep driving up to Billings."

"Or try harder to meet someone here in town. Maybe you should talk to Maisie."

"Surely you jest." Damien shot his brother an incredulous look. "I can't ask my sister to help me find a bed partner."

"True. Though you could ask her to help you get a few dates, you know. It's all in the way you put it. Since we were meeting for lunch today, I invited her to meet us here. She said something about you taking her Christmas shopping."

Damien groaned. "She's been hounding me about that."

"Then I guess now would be a good time to get started."

"What about you?" Damien leaned forward. "Maybe you should take her shopping. How much of your holiday shopping have you gotten done?"

As Wes was about to speak again, his fiancée, Lily Masterson, rushed up and interrupted, leaning in to give him a long, lingering and very public kiss.

Wes shot Damien a look that plainly said, *Speaking of sex...* Damn his hide. He might find this funny, but to Damien, it was no laughing matter. All he could do was clench his teeth and try to appear pleasant. "Hi Lily."

Her bright smile faltered a notch. "Hey, Damien."

Moving over so she could sit next to him, Wes draped his arm around Lily's slender shoulders before turning back to Damien. "Sorry. You were saying?"

Damien wanted to roll his eyes. Wes knew good and well he couldn't talk about this in front of Lily. Instead, he flashed her a quick smile. "Are you prepared for Christmas?"

As he'd suspected it would, the question sent her on a roll, listing what she'd bought and what she still needed to find and for whom.

Letting a clearly entranced Wes hang on to her every word, Damien tuned her out and slowly finished his beer. It was plain he wasn't going to get any help from his brother. He'd simply have to continue to find a woman on his own.

Again he thought of Eve Kelley and the kisses they'd shared. Just thinking of her heated his blood.

He wanted her. Though he claimed to be looking for a woman, any woman, right now only Eve Kelley would do.

Chapter 5

Watching through the window of Salon Allegra as the first snow flurries fluttered to the ground, Eve wiped a stray tear from her eye. Four months pregnant and already her hormones made her want to weep at the most inauspicious moments.

The approaching holidays made her feel even worse. She was alone and lonely, and because Honey Creek was such a small town, everyone knew. Most of the other women her age had families, some even had grandchildren. Most of them, especially the ones who hadn't been cheerleaders in high school, were either secretly glad about her situation or openly pitied her. On the edge of forty and still single! The shame!

Oddly enough, Eve herself hadn't really minded until the big four-oh had started to loom closer. She'd still had a sort of misguided faith that eventually the right man would come along. Which might explain why she'd been so eager to believe Massimo, with his honeyed promises and sensuous embrace.

Her mother, Bonnie Gene, kept bugging her to join the quilting group she'd started, refusing to let the minor fact that Eve had no interest in quilting deter her. Worse, despite her mom's promise, she knew she would continue to constantly network among her friends and in town, trying to set Eve up on one blind date after another.

So far, like the one last night with Gary, the dates had all been embarrassing disasters. Bonnie Gene refused to listen. She wanted grandbabies and would stop at nothing to get them.

If only she knew...

Eve rubbed her sore neck. Soon, she'd have her own little family of two. An unwed mother at thirty-nine. She couldn't help but wonder what her sister Susan would say. Recently engaged to Duke Colton, Susan had asked Eve to be one of her bridesmaids. Eve had agreed, but soon she'd have to ask Susan how she felt about having a pregnant bridesmaid in her wedding.

Despite her family and the fact that she'd grown up in Honey Creek, Eve had never felt so alone.

Turning away from the window, Eve turned up the thermostat and thought longingly of Italy's warm sunshine. She'd gone there alone on an impromptu vacation over the summer, and had met a sensuous Italian named Massimo. A chance encounter had turned into a whirlwind romance. Massimo had loved her for three wonderful, sun-drenched days before vanishing. She supposed she'd always understood a crazy fling like that would never last, that things had been too perfect to be real, but still...his disappearing act had hurt. She'd actually dared to believe that this time she'd found The One.

Instead, her infatuation had been just that. Starved for

attention, deprived of sex, she'd let physical attraction blind her to the fact that Massimo was a player. She'd come back to Honey Creek a little heart-sore, but wiser, completely unaware of the little life growing inside of her.

Now, nearly four months and three missed periods later, she knew she was pregnant with Massimo's child. Cupping her slightly rounded stomach, she paced the confines of her shop, marveling at the twist of fate that had brought her to this. She hadn't yet gotten used to the idea, despite having known for one month.

Part of her was mortified that, at nearly forty years old, she had gotten knocked up. She knew better and had, in fact, insisted on precautions.

Another part of her was secretly thrilled. Her own baby! Though the town—already a soap opera of gossip and intrigue with the whole Mark Walsh mess—would flay her alive with their wagging tongues, she was keeping this baby. She'd realized she might never find a man of her own. Who knew if she'd ever get a chance to have another baby? This son or daughter was hers. She'd be her child's sole parent, since all attempts to reach the man she'd known only by one name—Massimo—had been fruitless.

She wanted to celebrate, to revel in her pregnancy. Still, she kept it secret, not wanting to take away from Susan's wedding plans and the holiday. Plus, she wanted to enjoy the knowledge in private for as long as possible before becoming the object of pointing fingers and censuring eyes.

Her thoughts went to Damien. He'd certainly understand that. Though he'd been sent to prison through no fault of his own, the people of Honey Creek persisted in treating him like a pariah.

As they no doubt would treat her. Her body was changing. For now, she could hide that with loose clothing, but she wouldn't be able to hide it much longer.

She'd reveal her news in her own time. Until then, all of Eve's energy went toward appearing normal, at least until the holidays were over. Eventually, she'd have no choice but to go public, but for now, no one needed to know. Except... she flushed. Damien Colton. Why she'd revealed her secret to the one man who attracted her above all others, she didn't know.

The salon was quiet—too quiet. She'd finished all of her morning appointments and all the afternoon clients had cancelled due to the impending blizzard. Eve knew she should close down the salon and head home, but she couldn't seem to make herself move.

Just as she stirred enough to get up and go around shutting off lights and unplugging hair tools, her cell phone rang. It was her mother, inviting her to lunch at the Corner Bar. Since this would offer a respite from going home to her big, empty house and since the Corner Bar also served a mean burger, Eve agreed to meet Bonnie Gene in fifteen minutes.

Pulling on her down parka, she turned the sign on the door to Closed and went out into the swirling snow flurries. Though the weather wasn't bad now, with the blizzard in the forecast for that evening, everyone who'd remained in town was rushing around buying staples and trying to Christmas shop while they could.

The kind of snowfall being forecast could mean a complete shutdown of Honey Creek for a day or two, sometimes more if they lost power.

Eve wasn't worried. Even if she had forgotten to stock something at home, her pickup had four-wheel drive and she'd been driving in blizzards all her life.

Enjoying the pretty curtain of snow, she walked the

block and a half to the Corner Bar. A popular eating spot during the day and watering hole at night, the place was crowded, even for noon. Her family's barbecue restaurant was equally crowded, but no one in her family liked to go there except on special occasions. And when they did, they tended to close the back room. Otherwise, they were besieged by people wanting the secret recipe for their famous barbecue sauce.

Inside, she walked up to the hostess and requested a booth. Since they were all taken, she settled on a table near the back and out of the main footpath. She'd ordered a Shirley Temple, glad she got to give the order before her mom arrived. Watching the patterns the swirling fury of the snowfall made outside the windows, she fell into a daydream about decorating a nursery.

Fifteen minutes came and went. Her stomach rumbled a hungry protest, reminding her she was eating for two. Checking her watch for the third time, she sighed. Her mother was late again, which was a normal occurrence. Even the waitress had expected it and hadn't bothered her with requests to take her order.

Life in a small town. As she did every day, Eve reflected on how lucky she was to live here. Although she had enjoyed the cosmopolitan, old-world atmosphere in Europe, Montana would always be her home. She'd never been one of those who wanted to move somewhere else.

Twenty minutes crept past. Eve had her Shirley Temple refilled. Still no Bonnie Gene. She took to studying the menu, as though she didn't already have it memorized. Since she'd already decided on a hamburger and fries, she looked at the five different burger variations, trying to decide on which one.

The front door opened, sending a gust of icy air through the bar before it closed. The steady clatter of plates and glasses and people talking stilled for a second, then resumed again at an even louder roar. Eve glanced up and she felt a jolt go through her like a shockwave. For a second she forgot to breath and her heart skipped a beat.

Him. Looking as tall, dark and dangerous as a demon straight out of hell, Damien Colton strode into the room, drawing everyone's stare. He, of course, looked neither left nor right, pushing through the crowd like a broad-shouldered linebacker. For a moment, she thought she'd forgotten their date, but then realized it was far too early in the day for that.

As she had the night before, she contemplated how he'd changed. Prison had altered him a lot, she supposed. The earlier promise of his sulky beauty had matured, sharpened into a sort of rugged masculinity. He'd beefed up, no doubt from working out while behind bars, and if he'd ever had that prison pallor, the last three months he'd spent working on his family's cattle ranch had darkened his skin to bronze. Even the overcast skies of winter hadn't done much to dim his tan.

He was, she thought, absolutely, breathtakingly beautiful in a far different way than Massimo had been.

Dangerous for a woman like her. If she was smart, she'd stay far, far away from him. She didn't need that kind of trouble. Her hand drifted to her belly. Especially not now.

Still unable to look away, she sucked in her breath as he glanced over his shoulder, his dark gaze locking on hers.

Damn. Hurriedly, she looked down, cheeks flaming. Then, peeping up through her lashes, she watched as Damien took a seat across the room in a booth with his brother Wes. As he sat, the crowd of people obscured him from her view. Grateful he hadn't come over—heaven help her explain that one to her mother—part of her felt hurt that he'd ignored her.

Still, it took a while for her racing heart to settle back into a steady beat.

"Hey there, girl." Bonnie Gene breezed up, grabbing Eve in a fierce hug before she'd even had time to register her mother's arrival.

"Have you ordered yet?" Dropping into the seat across from Eve, Bonnie Gene snatched up the menu and flipped it open.

"Not yet." Eve couldn't keep her gaze from straying over toward the side of the bar where Damien sat.

Naturally, Bonnie Gene noticed. "What are you looking at?" Then, without waiting for an answer, she pushed to her feet to get a better look. "Damien Colton. I'll be."

Eve felt her face heat. Dang it.

"Hmmm." Her mother's shrewd blue eyes pinned Eve. "I feel really bad about what happened to that boy. Have you spoken to him yet?"

That boy was now thirty-five, and whether Eve had talked to him was none of her mother's business. Still, she couldn't outright lie. "A little, just in passing."

"I haven't. But I have talked to his sister. Just yesterday, in fact."

"You talked to Maisie Colton?" Surprised, Eve stared. Everyone in Honey Creek knew how much Maisie hated the Kelleys. Each and every single one of them. "When? How'd you manage to get her to talk to you? Was she... nice?"

Bonnie Gene signaled the waitress, who hurried over with a steaming cup of coffee, her usual drink, even in a bar. "Yesterday. And yes, she was nice. She's the one who approached me."

"Why?"

"She wants to join the quilting group."

Eve's mouth fell open. She couldn't have been more surprised if her mother had suddenly announced she wanted to take up hang-gliding. "Really?"

"Yes, really." Satisfied with her daughter's stunned reaction, the older woman sat back in her chair, smiled and sipped her coffee. "She's supposed to come visit our meeting next Thursday night. You ought to come, too. It'll be fun."

For once, Eve actually considered attending. But she knew if she started going now, her mother would expect her to go forever and always. Still, watching the train wreck of Maisie Colton trying to interact with a bunch of fervent quilters made it awfully tempting.

"Does she even know how to quilt?"

"I don't know." Supremely unconcerned, Bonnie shrugged. "If she doesn't, we'll teach her. It's about time that woman started trying to become a part of her community."

"Maisie Colton?" Eve couldn't wrap her mind around the image of long-legged, willowy, model-perfect Maisie Colton trying to make a quilt with her own exquisitely manicured fingers. "I hope this doesn't come back to bite you."

The waitress hurried over to take their orders. Eve ordered the California burger, with avocado and bean sprouts. After a second of consideration, her mother ordered the same.

After the waitress left, Bonnie Gene leaned across the table. "Are you going to go talk to him?"

"What? Who?"

"Damien Colton. You always did have a thing for him."

"Mother!" Horrified, Eve glanced around to see who might have heard. "I did not."

"Don't think I didn't know how you mooned over him when you were in high school."

Eve rolled her eyes. One fact of life—no matter how old she got, her mother could still make her feel like a little kid. "Drop it, Mom. Please."

Chuckling, Bonnie nodded. "Have it your way." About to say something else, she broke into a wide smile, jumped to her feet and began waving madly. "Well, look who's here. Maisie Colton. Yoo-hoo, Maisie! Over here!"

Instantly, the Corner Bar went silent. Voices hushed, forks stilled as all heads turned to stare at the door. Tall and statuesque, Maisie glided toward them. Her four-inch heels tap-tapping on the wooden floor was the only sound in the place.

For the second time that day, Eve wanted to let the ground swallow her up. Instead, since she had no choice, she lifted her chin, forced a pleasant smile and watched Maisie approach.

One thing about those Coltons, she thought. They were all lookers. With her exotically tilted aquamarine eyes, and perfect figure, Maisie would draw stares whether in New York, Paris or Bozeman, Montana. The hairdresser in Eve eyed the long, thick, brown hair cascading down Maisie's back, and longed to work with it. Since Maisie traveled to Billings once a month to have her hair done, she knew that would never happen. Eve's Salon Allegra was far too plebian for the likes of Maisie Colton.

"Bonnie Gene!" With a genuine grin on her bright-red lips, Maisie enveloped Bonnie Gene in a hug. "So good to see you."

"Come, join us." Scooting over, Bonnie patted the seat next to her. "I'm sure you know my daughter, Eve."

"I've seen you around, but I don't believe we've ever formally met." Maisie's smile turned cool as she held her perfectly manicured hand for Eve to shake. "You were a year behind me in high school."

"Pleased to meet you," Eve lied, suddenly overwhelmingly conscious of her short, unpainted fingernails.

They touched hands quickly, and Maisie sat down.

Luckily, Bonnie Gene kept the conversation rolling, and soon Maisie was chatting about everything from cattle wandering off in a blizzard to the latest winter fashions.

Meanwhile, Eve kept watching the kitchen while her stomach rumbled, waiting for her food.

Finally, the hamburgers arrived, dropped off by the hostess, as their waitress was busy waiting on other tables. Eve reached for her burger, ignoring Maisie's stare of disapproval as she raised it to her mouth and took a huge bite.

Heaven. It was all she could do to keep from rolling her eyes and moaning out loud.

Bonnie Gene, however, was a bit more gracious. "Maisie, would you like half of mine? We ordered long before you came in."

"No, thanks," Maisie drawled. "I don't eat beef."

That was too much, even for Eve. Swallowing her food, she couldn't resist pointing out. "Um, Maisie? You live on a cattle ranch."

Up went one perfectly shaped brow. "So?"

Staring at her, Eve tried to picture Darius Colton's reaction to a daughter who wouldn't eat beef. The autocratic cattleman had never been shy in proclaiming his contempt and disdain for what he called 'tree huggers' and 'vegans.' Was this her way of rebelling against an autocratic and dictatorial father? If so, Maisie was now a bit too old to be still playing that sort of game.

Either way, it wasn't Eve's business. "I just thought it was different, that's all. While I admire you for your principles, I could never do it. I love my meat too much."

"I can tell." Maisie let her gaze sweep disparagingly over Eve. Then, while Eve was still reeling from the incredibly rude comment—standard Maisie Colton— Maisie continued. "The way you're eating that burger it's almost like you're eating for two or something."

Eve froze. Panicked, she looked at her mother, to see Bonnie Gene also staring slack-jawed at the crazy Colton woman.

Blithely, as though completely unaware she'd said anything wrong, Maisie kept on. "Of course, you've got to actually have a man to get pregnant, and since everyone knows you're not dating anyone, unless you used a sperm bank or something—"

"Maisie!" Bonnie Gene barked, cutting her off. "I think that's enough. I'm shocked at your behavior."

Right. As if her mother had reason to be surprised. Maisie Colton would never change. Maisie was…Maisie. Beautiful, spoiled, unbalanced. She'd been that way as long as Eve could remember.

Yet, at Bonnie Gene's words, unbelievably, the glamorous Colton ducked her head, appearing contrite. "My apologies," she said, stiffly. "I meant no harm."

A shadow fell over their table. Damien Colton, grim-faced and impossibly handsome. "Ladies."

Eve's heart rate went into overdrive. His gaze touched on Eve, again briefly, sending a jolt directly to her insides. "Maisie, Wes and I are waiting for you over there. Lily's joined us as well." Holding out his hand for his sister, he waited patiently while Maisie made up her mind.

"I was meeting you for lunch, wasn't I?" she said in a sheepish tone, wrinkling her perfect nose prettily. "I'm so sorry I kept you waiting. I wanted to talk to Bonnie Gene for a second. She's going to teach me how to quilt."

To his credit, Damien didn't react to this news at all. He simply nodded, taking her hand and helping his sister to her feet.

"Sorry to interrupt your lunch, Ms. Kelley. Eve." This time, as his gaze met hers, Eve saw the hint of a promise in his. While she still tried to figure that out, he began to move off, Maisie on his arm.

"By the way," he said, glancing over his broad shoulder at her. "Do I need an appointment to get a haircut at that salon of yours, or can I just drop in?"

For one horrifying moment, Eve couldn't find her voice. Pulling it back somehow from somewhere, she managed a response. "How about Tuesday afternoon? Around four?"

He dipped his chin to acknowledge her words. "I'll be there." Then, with his sister's arm tucked in his, he left them.

Wow. Eve couldn't keep herself from watching him until the crowd blocked her view. "I've never cut a Colton man's hair," she breathed. "They usually go to the Old Time Barber Shop down the street. I can't believe this."

"Get your tongue back in your mouth, girl," Bonnie teased as she finally wrapped her hands around her burger.

"I know," Eve sighed. "Damien Colton's one kind of trouble I don't need." She'd need to keep reminding herself of that. Especially since every time she saw him, she turned to Jell-O inside.

"So," Maisie asked brightly, clutching Damien's arm as though she needed help to stay upright. Hell, trying to walk with those high-heeled boots, she probably did. "Are you ready to do some serious Christmas shopping?"

They'd reached the booth and the flurry of hellos and hugs saved Damien from answering. Maisie was the only one who acted as though he hadn't changed. She still treated him as if he was the same twenty-year-old boy who'd gone away to prison for fifteen years. As if she was trying to pretend that his long incarceration had never happened.

She and she alone appeared blind to how he'd changed. She didn't understand that he was different, that he'd become a bitter, angry man. Though he hated that, he accepted it, hoping with time some of the bitterness would fade. The only time he found any peace was on the back of a horse, riding the land, far away from people or buildings or anything even remotely resembling civilization.

But not only had Maisie been nagging him to go Christmas shopping with her, but he'd needed to meet up with Wes. As Honey Creek's sheriff, Wes was swamped at what normally was the slowest time of the year. With the Mark Walsh investigation going full-swing and the FBI in town, Wes hadn't been able to make time to get out to the ranch.

Fifteen years ago, a dead body had been mistakenly identified as Mark Walsh and Damien had been convicted of his murder. Then, some months ago, when the real Mark Walsh turned up actually dead and Damien had been exonerated, the search was on for his real killer.

Worse, the FBI had been in town. Damien had actually spoken to one of the agents again a while back, agreeing to help in the investigation any way he could. What he hadn't realized was that the Feds were in town for another reason, besides Mark Walsh's murder. They were looking into some of Darius Colton's business deals and had begun pressuring Damien to help them out. Not a day went by that he didn't regret his impulsive offer to help, especially since they were increasing the pressure.

Damien couldn't care less what his father might have done by making the wrong investment or whatever. The last thing Darius needed was to go to prison for some white-collar crime—Damien knew firsthand what prison could do to a man. And Darius was sixty—if he went behind bars now, he'd probably never get out. No, thank you. Damien wanted nothing to do with that mess. All he cared about was finding Mark Walsh's real killer. And, of course, finding out what had happened to his inheritance.

He had been hopeful Wes could fill him in on the investigation, hopeful they'd made real progress. He had a keen interest in finding out both who had actually finally killed Mark, and the identity of the body he had been accused of murdering fifteen years ago. Someone had killed that guy, whoever he was. Damien wondered what the tie-in was to the real Mark Walsh.

Had Mark set up the first killing, faking his own death? Surely he'd known Damien had taken the fall for his death and gone away to do hard jail time.

But evidently, Mark hadn't cared. People had believed him dead. Dead, he'd been free as a bird, while Damien's entire life had been ruined.

Nothing and no one could ever give Damien back what had been taken from him. Now, the burning drive to know the truth and a lack of ready funds were the only things that kept Damien in town.

Until his father had told him flatly that his inheritance was gone, he'd planned his entire future around that money. This, combined with the money his attorney said that the State of Montana would be paying him for his wrongful conviction, would be enough to start his own cattle ranch far away from Honey Creek. Someplace like Nevada or

Idaho. He'd already started pricing acreage, preparing himself for when he could shake the dust of this place from his heels.

Honey Creek, Montana, held nothing for him anymore. Nothing but painful memories. Except now that he had no inheritance, it looked like he was being held prisoner. Again.

Chapter 6

"Hellooo? Earth to Damien?" Maisie's voice, plus her fingers snapping in front of his face, brought him back to the Corner Bar.

"Sorry." He gave his older sister a rueful smile, noticing how Wes and Lily still couldn't tear their gazes away from each other. Love. Bitterness filled him. "What'd you need?"

"I asked if you were ready to go lighten your wallet after we eat?"

His wallet was already pretty damn light, but he didn't tell her that. The wage his father paid him for working on the ranch was the same as he paid all the other ranch hands. Not exactly a fortune. "Yes, I'm ready to go Christmas shopping," he lied.

She grinned, making his small falsehood worth the trouble. Just because he wasn't feeling Christmassy didn't mean he had to ruin the holiday for her.

They took their seats, Damien letting Maisie slide in first, so he could have the outside of the booth. Even before his prison experience, he hadn't liked feeling hemmed in. Now, if he wasn't careful, he'd feel trapped.

"Good. Shopping's my thing. Now, we've got to plan." Rummaging in her oversized purse, she produced a small pad of paper and a shiny silver Montblanc pen.

"Plan? Can't we just go?"

"Not when we've got as much to buy as you do," she chided. "Now let's see. I'm making a list of places we need to stop by." Scribbling furiously, oblivious to everyone else, she began plotting.

Damien exchanged a glance with Wes, who shrugged. Lily caught this and punched him lightly in the arm. Meanwhile, Maisie continued writing, unaware.

Finally, she raised her head and pushed the paper toward Damien. "Take a look. I think this will cover everything, unless there is someplace you want to add?"

Eying the paper, Damien groaned. "There must be ten different stores on this list," he groused, earning Wes's sympathetic grin. "Isn't there one place we can go and get everything? Like one-shop stopping?"

"The nearest Wally World is in Bozeman. That's twenty minutes away in good weather. With this snowstorm that's supposed to hit tonight, I think we'd better stay in town."

"That's pretty sensible," Lily agreed. She sounded surprised, which made Maisie grin. People outside the family saw only her eccentric, off-balance behavior. They'd been witness to enough emotional roller-coaster rides to label her crazy, which Damien could understand. Even in the short time he'd been home, he'd come to realize that his sister had some serious psychological issues.

Personally, he wondered if she might be bipolar. In that case, she'd be fine with the right medications. But the one time Damien had brought up the topic with their father, Darius had gone ballistic and the subject had been dropped.

So poor Maisie flew high and frequently dived low enough to scrape bottom. The entire town thought she was crazy. Damien believed she was actually sick. One thing he firmly intended to do before leaving Honey Creek was get Maisie the help she needed, even if he had to go against his father to do so. Thus far, though he'd been trying for the past few months, he hadn't had any luck. Maisie herself refused even to consider the possibility of seeking medical help.

Damn. Not for the first time, he reflected how complicated life was on the outside. Had he really believed when he'd been set free that he could go back to the simple days of riding the range and minding cattle?

"Damien?"

Again he raised his head to find everyone at the table eyeing him quizzically.

"You drifted off again," Maisie complained.

"Are you all right, bro?" Wes asked, concern furrowing his brow.

"Fine. Just tired. I was up all night with that sick cow."

Wes shook his head. "I'm so glad I don't have to do that stuff anymore."

"I missed it," Damien said simply.

"Yeah, out of all us kids, you and Duke were the only two who took to cattle-ranching. The rest of us didn't want anything to do with it."

"I agree." Maisie shook her head, sending her long hair flying and her huge, dangling earrings tinkling. "Nasty, smelly animals. I don't even like being in the same area as them."

This made the brothers both laugh.

"I can't even remember the last time you went to the barn," Wes said.

"I've been home almost four months and she hasn't been near the place in all that time," Damien seconded.

Lily reached across the table and lightly touched the back of Maisie's hand. "I don't blame you. Cattle are hell on manicures."

They all got a chuckle out of that, though the women didn't seem to understand why the men found this so amusing.

The waitress brought their food on a huge, circular tray. Damien realized with surprise that while he'd been woolgathering, Wes had evidently ordered them all burgers and fries, except for Maisie, of course, who had a huge bowl of broccoli-cheese soup and a small salad.

For the life of him, Damien couldn't understand how anyone could eat that way, but his sister made her own choices. If she wanted to be a vegetarian, who was he to judge?

He picked up his burger. The meat had been piled high with crispy bacon and mushrooms and cheese and smelled as close to heaven as a meal could. He dug in with gusto. Silence finally fell while the others did the same.

For some reason, while he ate his thoughts returned to Eve Kelley, sitting with her mother and Maisie earlier. God, she was beautiful. Each time he saw her he felt that familiar pull in his gut, signaling his desire. When she'd met his gaze, he'd recognized something in her face. As fanciful as it sounded, her eyes had looked...haunted. He knew haunted. Intimately.

"Maisie, I didn't know you and Eve Kelley were friends," he said into the silence.

Both Wes and Lily stopped chewing and stared.

Maisie scowled. "We're not. I told you, Bonnie Gene is going to teach me to quilt. I'm going to the first meeting this week, if we aren't snowed in."

Wes asked the obvious. "Why do you want to learn to quilt?"

At his question, Maisie's expression grew serious and determined. "For Jeremy. I want to make my son a quilt, so he'll have something to remember me by when I'm gone."

Concerned, Damien exchanged a glance with his brother. "Maisie, are you planning on going somewhere?"

She bit her lip, twisting the huge diamond ring that she always wore on her right hand. "No. You know what I mean. Someday we all die, right?"

Relieved, he squeezed her shoulder. "Someday. Just not any time soon, all right?"

"Of course." Then, in her usual way, she changed moods. From somber to giddy, lightning-swift. "I'm so excited about Christmas! I can't wait to get my gifts purchased and everything wrapped!"

He noticed Lily's wide-eyed stare. Though she and Wes were engaged, she obviously hadn't been around Maisie enough to get used to her.

Picking up his burger again, he nudged his sister. "And we'd better eat up so we can get started on all this shopping."

Munching happily, she nodded.

A short while later, food devoured, small talk dispensed with and heartily sick and tired of watching Wes and Lily hang all over each other, Damien and Maisie donned their heavy parkas and exited the Corner Bar.

It took every bit of self-restraint he possessed to keep from glancing over to see if Eve Kelley and her mother were still there. He could still remember her locked in his arms that night in the cab of his pickup. She'd been hot and willing and soft and beautiful.

Like a dash of cold water, he remembered that more than sixteen years had passed since that night. For him, it might seem like yesterday. But Eve would definitely have moved on.

Except she was still alone. And he wanted her.

Outside, the icy air and blowing snow hit him like a welcome slap in the face. Maisie kept hold of his arm.

"I love this time of the year," she enthused. "Look at all the beautiful decorations."

He squinted where she pointed, trying to make out what she meant. "All I can see is the snow. It's already a couple of inches deep."

"Spoilsport." Punching his arm, she began to sing "Jingle Bells," then stopped in mid verse to glare at him. "Feel free to join in at any time."

"I'm only here because of you," he groused.

"That and the fact that Christmas is only ten days away and you haven't bought a single gift. Sing along. Christmas songs might help you get in the spirit."

"I doubt that. You know I can't carry a tune."

A group of people, bundled in down coats and wearing knitted hats and scarves, hurriedly crossed the street to avoid them.

"Did you see that?" Damien glared after them. "The way people act makes me want to punch something."

"Just ignore them." Tottering along in her high-heeled, pointy-toed boots, Maisie used his arm like a lifeline. "People here always treat me like I have a disease. So, for sure, they'll treat you the same. Like prison's catching or somethin'." She giggled loudly at her own joke.

Even Damien had to smile. At least Maisie hadn't changed, other than growing older. She was the same eccentric wild child now as she had been when he went into prison, albeit now she was a grown woman with a teenage son.

"Besides," she continued. "Who cares what the townspeople think? You don't need to worry about them. You have us. You have family."

"True." That was the one rock-solid thing he'd hung on to while incarcerated. His family. Unlike most of the other inmates, he'd always have family. He'd known, despite their failure to win his freedom, that he could count on them. He knew they'd all tried to fight his conviction, knew they'd funneled money to various high-powered attorneys trying to force an appeal. They'd never doubted his innocence, or him. They'd had faith in him, which had given him faith in himself.

Everyone, that is, except his father. Though he'd harbored a bit of bitterness toward Darius Colton for not trying harder to get him free, Damien had emerged from prison ready to start over, forgive and forget and all that. But the passing years had not been kind to the patriarch of the Colton clan. Darius had grown colder, more autocratic, secretive and unreasonable. Of all the family, Damien felt, his father had become a stranger.

And after the incident last night, a mentally unsound stranger at that. Who might have stolen his own children's inheritance.

"Stop being a grinch and enjoy the holiday. Now, what's important today is getting your gifts," she reiterated, fluffing the snowflakes out of her long, dark hair and grinning up at him. "Especially the one you're buying me."

"Buying?" he teased. "I was going to make you something."

She pouted and he relented. Maisie knew he only had

the small paycheck his father allotted him for working on the ranch.

"Just don't be too extravagant, okay?"

"I won't." The mischief in her violet eyes told him she had something up her sleeve. "Though you could always charge it. That's what makes plastic so fun."

"You know I can't." He hadn't even bothered to apply for a credit card, not seeing a point since he'd planned to pay cash for everything once he got his inheritance.

Again he wondered why his father had dodged questions about that.

"I've lost you again," Maisie pouted. "Come on, Damien. It's not like I get you all to myself very often. Can you at least try to pay attention?"

Pushing all troubling thoughts out of his head, Damien forced himself to relax. "Sorry, sis. It won't happen again."

"Good."

Thirty minutes later, while the snow continued to fall in thick, wet flakes and pile up on the ground, Damien struggled to the car with his third load of parcels. Maisie's, all of them. She'd gone a little crazy once she got started, though since a good portion of her gifts were for Jeremy, he couldn't fault her.

He'd purchased exactly two things—a purple cashmere sweater that Maisie swore she couldn't live without, and the latest video-game console with two games for Jeremy. He made sure there were two controllers so they could play together.

"You still have Duke and Susan, Finn, Wes and Lily, not to mention Darius and Sharon. And Perry, Joan and Brand, of course."

"You're right," he said slowly. Though he was on the fence about Darius, he did need to get a gift for his father's wife. Though he barely knew the woman, third or so in a long line of wraithlike females who allowed themselves to be totally domineered by Darius, she'd always been civil to him. "What do you think I should get Sharon?"

"She likes scarves," Maisie pointed out. "What are you going to get Darius?"

"I'm not sure. I'm going to wait on getting him anything right now."

To his relief, she accepted that. "Okay. Then what about our brothers?"

"For the guys, I figured the feed store would have everything I need."

"The feed store?" Her expression mirrored her mock horror. "Surely you're kidding."

"I wasn't."

"You'd better be. Come on, you've got to get started. You've bought hardly anything," Maisie complained.

He stopped in his tracks, tightening his grip on her arm to keep her from falling. "You want to know something? I'm not sure about even celebrating Christmas," he teased. "Fifteen years in prison without the holiday made me kind of used to doing without it."

She slapped his arm with her purse, a huge, gaudy thing that seemed comprised of fake rattlesnake dyed a rainbow of colors, some natural, some not. "You are definitely celebrating Christmas, and you'll be happy about it. I insist. No arguing."

He hid a smile. "Yes, ma'am," he drawled.

"Here we are." She stopped in front of the Honey Creek Mercantile. "Our next stop. You should be able to get a little something for everyone here."

Since it was either that or listen to her complain, Damien nodded and pulled open the door, holding it for his sister and trying like hell not to notice how everyone in the store suddenly became busy doing something else. Something that made it impossible for him to catch their eyes.

Once again he stopped in his tracks, forgetting Maisie still clutched his arm and nearly causing her to fall.

"What's wrong now?" she asked.

Gesturing around the place, he shook his head. "I know you claim it doesn't bother you, but it does me."

"What does?" she asked, appearing honestly perplexed.

"This." Gesturing toward the packed store, he shook his head. "The way they act like I have a communicable disease."

"You'll be fine." Her firm, no-nonsense voice told him if she willed him to be fine, then he would. "Honestly, don't let them bother you."

"Easy for you to say. Coming to town makes me feel more like a criminal than prison did."

Maisie shot him a sideways glance. "It's not going to change any time soon, so get used to it."

He stopped, staring down at her. "That's where you're wrong, Maisie. I don't have to get used to it. And, like I've told you before, I'm leaving and you're welcome to come with me when I go."

Shaking her head, she only smiled and continued shopping.

After she'd finished her lunch with her mother, Eve switched her truck to four-wheel drive, glad she already had her snow chains on, and headed home, reveling in the bright white silence of the falling snow. Soon, if the storm gathered the strength the weathermen predicted, there'd be whiteout conditions, and no one would be going anywhere. But for now, it was a pretty typical Montana snowfall. Pretty, but nothing to get excited about.

At the house, she let Max, her boxer, out, smiling as the big, goofy fawn-colored dog bounded about, trying to catch the flakes in his mouth, whirling and bouncing and rolling in the snow. Watching him, with her gloved hands cradled protectively over her stomach, her worries fell away as if they'd never existed.

She smiled, her heart full. This dog was good for her soul.

The snowfall, now just a normal winter storm, was supposed to intensify as the night went on, eventually becoming a full-out blizzard, what the locals called a blue norther. A common enough occurrence in Montana in December. She had plenty of firewood, a pantry stocked full of food, and she wouldn't have to worry if she couldn't get into town to replenish her supplies.

Max bounded up, tail wagging, reminding her with a soft woof that it was his supper time.

"Come on, boy."

Inside, she poured the big dog a bowl of kibble. She kept an extra thirty-pound bag for occasions like this.

While her dog feasted, she found herself again thinking about Damien Colton. His aloof loneliness acted like an invisible lure, making her want to get closer.

Bad, bad Eve.

Still, she knew he had no friends. Everyone could use a friend and she was lonely. What would be the harm in that?

So she decided later to head into town and stop by the Corner Bar for a drink, despite the impending blizzard. Weather forecasts were often wrong and if they weren't, any Montana native worth their salt could drive in a snowstorm. If Damien was there, she'd join him.

She chose to ignore the fact that her heart rate accelerated at the thought.

* * *

"You're going back into town?" Maisie sounded incredulous. "We've only been back a few hours and you bitched the entire time we were there."

Before Damien could answer, Jeremy jumped up.

"Can I go with you, Uncle Damien?"

Gazing down into his nephew's bright eyes, Damien Colton glanced at his sister, Maisie. Her intense aqua gaze unfocused, she shrugged, in her own careless way giving permission.

Unfortunately, no way in hell he was bringing his fourteen-year-old nephew to a bar, even one like the Corner Bar and Grill.

"Not this time," Damien said. "Snow's on the way."

"So?" Maisie drawled. "Since when do we let a little snow stop us?"

"Maybe next time." Damien felt guilty disappointing his nephew, but he had no choice.

"Why not?" Jeremy challenged. "Mom gave me some money. I've got to get my Christmas shopping done, too."

"I'm not going shopping," Damien answered. "Sorry."

Maisie perked up at that. "Then where are you going?"

"Out for a drink." He squeezed his nephew's shoulder. Though he'd rather be dragged over broken glass than go shopping again, he had to do something to wipe the disappointment from the kid's face. "I'll take you tomorrow after school, okay?"

Jeremy nodded. "That'll work. I've got homework to do tonight anyway." Pushing back his chair, he got up and wandered off.

"He idolizes you, you know," Maisie pointed out, still absorbed in painting her fingernails a bright scarlet, apparently to match the cashmere sweater she wore.

"Ever since you got out of prison, all he ever talks about is you."

Damien frowned. "He has better examples in Duke, Wes and Finn."

Smiling, Maisie glanced toward the den at the twelve-foot-tall Christmas tree. Decked out all in silver and white with twinkling lights, the tree appeared to glow. "I don't know about that. I trust my son's judgment. Just don't disappoint him, okay?"

"I won't." Of all the family, Jeremy was the person Damien most enjoyed being with.

"Now tell me." Maisie cocked her head, eyeing him with interest. "Do you actually have a date or are you going trolling?"

"Trolling?"

"As in fishing. For a woman."

For half a second he thought of Wes saying he should ask Maisie to set him up. Just as quickly, he discounted that plan. Bad idea.

"Neither," he lied. "I'm simply going to town to have a drink. The Rollaboys are playing at the Corner Bar tonight."

"Oooh!" Maisie clapped her hands. "I can't believe I forgot that. I may go up there myself later."

Damn. Now he felt obligated to offer. "Do you want to go with me?"

She grinned. "No, but thanks for asking. I wouldn't want to cramp your style. Plus I want to make sure Darius isn't on the warpath. No way I'm leaving Jeremy here to fend for himself if our father is working into a good drunk."

"Smart move." He touched her arm. "Then I guess I'll be going."

"You'd stand a better chance of getting lucky if you drove up to Bozeman."

"I know." He raised a brow. "The question is, how did you know?"

Lifting one shoulder, she smiled. "You're not the only one with needs. None of the men in this town will date me."

"You seemed to be doing all right with that Gary Jackson."

"Oh, him." Her smile widened. "He's new in town and apparently doesn't believe all he hears. He and I have a date this Friday."

"Good for you."

"Yeah." Her smile tinged with sadness, she put the cap back on the bottle of nail polish. "I'll make it last as long as I can. Until I freak out over something and he takes off running."

"Maise." He touched the back of her hand. "Have you considered getting some help?"

Maisie's gaze slid away. "I don't need help," she muttered. "I'm a little moody, that's all. Leave me alone."

Before he could respond, she turned and stalked off.

Stalemate. Again.

He reminded himself he couldn't fix the world. Hell, he couldn't even repair his own problems—why did he think he could help anyone else?

Chapter 7

This Friday night was clear, crisp and cold. Eve drove into town feeling oddly reluctant, restless and not sure why. Since Damien Colton's handsome face kept popping into her mind, she figured the restlessness had a lot to do with her unfulfilled desire for him.

The parking lot was full. She lucked out into a spot near the entrance and parked, glad she'd taken extra care with her appearance.

At the door, she paused and surveyed the packed bar. Because she'd called ahead, the bartender had put a reserved sign on her regular booth and she headed for it, blowing him a kiss on her way.

Once he brought her Shirley Temple, Eve sat back and surveyed the scene. She waved at a family she knew as they snagged one of the last empty tables remaining. Unlike the other night, the bar was crowded. Even at 8:00 p.m., when the dinner rush would be beginning to die down, people milled in both the restaurant and around the bar area, elbow to elbow.

Tables were filling up fast. Tonight, the Rollaboys were playing. A local country-and-western band that had made good in Nashville, they'd returned home to visit family for the holidays and, following Honey Creek tradition, would play a free concert at the Corner Bar.

Since entertainment in their little town was pretty much limited to church nativity plays, ranchers and townspeople alike filled the room. The Rollaboys played an upbeat mix of country and rock that was enjoyed by all.

As the fifth person stopped by to chat with her, remarking excitedly on the band, Eve wondered if she should leave. She'd actually managed to forget the band was playing and would probably have stayed home if she'd remembered. She'd dated Ian Murphy, the Rollaboys' lead singer, on and off for two years a while back. The relationship had ended badly, with Eve refusing Ian's marriage proposal. She'd liked him well enough, and they were certainly compatible, but his lifestyle was the opposite of what she wanted for herself. She'd thought she'd been perfectly realistic, though Ian hadn't taken the breakup well.

She wondered if she should leave before Ian saw her. But the contrast between her big, empty house and the packed, boisterous bar was dramatic and she decided to stay. After all, it had been eighteen months since the breakup. Surely Ian had moved on by now. Deciding to stay, she settled back in her booth, hoping the shadows would keep her out of view of the stage.

Used to Eve's solitary ways, everyone waved and continued on to meet their group. A few people stopped by to chat briefly, but no one asked if they could join her.

Glad to be seated alone, Eve couldn't help but watch the door for Damien.

The waitress brought her another Shirley Temple. Eve found ordering them amusing since she associated them with Christmas. As a child, Bonnie Gene had served them to the Kelley kids in crystal wineglasses, always with a cherry as garnish. Eve planned to continue this tradition with her child when he or she was old enough.

The thought was enough to make her misty-eyed. Looking down at the table, she dabbed her eyes with her napkin, knowing she had to regain her composure quickly before someone noticed.

"Enjoying your Shirley Temple?"

The deep voice jolted Eve right out of her melancholy. She looked up and met Damien Colton's velvet-brown eyes. To her disbelief, she blushed and her heart skipped a beat.

"It's a seven and seven," she corrected out of habit, then realized as his smile widened that she'd said exactly the same thing the last time they'd met. Now he knew the truth. Had it been only yesterday?

"Mind if I join you?" he asked.

Her insides fluttered as she seriously considered his question. She glanced around, aware that the second he sat down the gossip would start. Finally, she shrugged. "Sure, why not?"

"Worried someone will see you talking to me?" He remained standing, balanced on the balls of his feet as though he meant to flee.

"Maybe." She owed him honesty, at least. "But not for the reason you think. Sit."

He studied her face for a moment, then slid into the booth across from her. "You really don't care?"

"They're going to gossip no matter what, so why not give them something to talk about?" Finding herself smiling, she leaned back in the booth. She realized she liked the way he made her feel. The sizzle of desire combined with a comforting sense of connection.

He smiled back, warming her down to the soles of her feet. "Aren't you worried about what they'll say?"

"Not really. Besides, even if you were Maisie, they'd talk. Because you're a Colton and I'm a Kelley, you know? Though I confess, I never actually bought into that whole feud thing like your sister did."

His smile dimmed. "Not only that. They're not going to like you sitting with me."

"Why not?"

"Because I'm an ex-con."

Incredulous, she could only stare. "Everyone knows you were exonerated. Mark Walsh wasn't even really dead."

"Someone was," he said grimly. "And though they used circumstantial evidence to convict me of a crime I didn't commit, no one seems to care about who the actual dead guy was or who killed him."

"Ah." She leaned forward, her earlier discomfort completely forgotten. "But you want to know."

"You'd better believe I do." Signaling the waitress, he held up his empty beer bottle. "I can't help but wonder if Mark Walsh himself set up the killing so he could disappear."

"That makes sense." Fascinated, she leaned forward. "But why? And now that Mark Walsh really is dead— fifteen years later—everyone is wondering who killed him this time."

"At least they can't pin it on me this time. I was already behind bars."

Impulsively, she reached across the table and laid her hand over his. "I'm so sorry. That must have been awful."

For a moment he simply stared at her, his expression

dark and unreadable. Abruptly, he stood, pulling his hand away as if her touch burned him. "It was. That's why as soon as I can, I'm leaving town. Excuse me," he growled. "I'll be right back."

Leaving town? She watched him cross the room, his masculine stride forceful and, if she admitted the truth to herself, sexy as hell. But then, even back in high school, she'd always had a thing for Damien Colton. Even her mom had been able to see that.

She smiled to herself at the memory. She'd been one of the popular kids, a cheerleader and a senior when she'd turned a corner with an armload of books and crashed into him. The attraction had been instant and hot and it hadn't seemed to matter a bit that Damien was a lowly freshman. She'd had a secret crush on him. Apparently, Damien hadn't felt the same. Of course, at the time, she'd been dating Mike Straum, the ex-quarterback of the football team. Kind of intimidating to anyone, even a Colton. Not to mention that Damien had started seeing Lucy Walsh.

Except one night at a field party, she'd had too much to drink and somehow, gloriously, she and Damien had ended up in the backseat of his truck.

When Damien had been arrested for Mark Walsh's murder, she'd been stunned and had protested loudly and often. Finally, Bonnie Gene took her aside and explained she wasn't helping Damien by complaining. If she truly believed him innocent, then she needed to try and figure out a way she could actually help him.

But someone else wanted Damien Colton convicted quickly. The trial had steamrolled on and he'd been railroaded right into prison. Then, the only thing Eve had been able to do was write him a letter, asking him if she could come visit.

Damien had never responded. Eve had decided to go visit him anyway, but Bonnie Gene persuaded her not to.

She'd always regretted that.

Still, moving away? She guessed the ever-present censure of their small town had proven too much for him.

Damien returned, sliding into the booth across from her and pinning her with his gaze. "Where were we?"

"We were talking about the murders."

"Yes. You asked why Mark Walsh would fake his own death. I think when they find that out, a lot of the other pieces will fall into place. But right now, no one seems to know. Not even my own brother, and he's the sheriff."

"Look on the bright side. At least you're lucky enough to have a brother who *is* the sheriff. That way, you'll find out as soon as they learn anything."

"Pollyanna," he mocked softly. "Are you always so upbeat?"

"So I've been told. I tend to wear rose-colored glasses. That's one of my biggest faults."

His gaze locked with hers. After a moment, he laughed. "You don't even sound too upset about that. So tell me, Ms. Glass-half-full-kind-of-person. What brings you out to the Corner Bar on yet another cold, snowy night?"

"I'm a barfly," she said flippantly, trying to get her stomach to quit doing somersaults inside her. "I hang out in bars because that's what I do."

"No, you're not. If you were a real barfly, you'd be constantly on the prowl for men."

"Maybe that's what I'm doing with you," she teased back.

Staring at her, his eyes darkened. Immediately after tossing off the words, she wished she could call them back. She used to be so good at flirting. Apparently, she'd completely lost her touch. And why did she want to flirt with Damien Colton anyway?

"Dangerous territory." His low, deep growl confirming her thought should have made her want to back off, but instead, it thrilled her in some deep, visceral way.

As she searched her mind for a response, a loud guitar riff sounded and the bartender stepped up to the microphone.

"Ladies and gentlemen, put your hands together and welcome home our friends the Rollaboys!"

The room erupted in cheers.

The music made talking at less than a shout impossible, so, as the dance floor filled, Eve sat back and enjoyed the music. She took care to stay in the shadows, ensuring that Ian couldn't see her and making sure not to make eye contact with him.

The first two songs were rollicking, boot-stomping numbers. After Ian addressed the crowd, the band segued into a slow, romantic ballad, making Eve sigh. "One Heart Too Heavy" had always been one of her favorites.

"Eve?"

Suddenly, she realized that Damien had gotten to his feet and now stood beside her.

Leaning in close, he spoke directly into her ear, his warm breath tickling her and making her shiver.

"Care to dance?" He held out his hand.

She eyed the mass of bodies swaying to the steel guitar. Suddenly, she didn't care if Ian saw her, if anyone saw her. She wanted Damien. Wanted to be held in Damien's muscular arms, to feel his broad chest against her cheek. The town would talk, Ian would most likely notice her, but she realized she actually didn't care.

For an answer, she slipped her hand into his and let him pull her out onto the dance floor.

* * *

Intensely aware of his unruly body, Damien briefly cursed himself for his foolishness. He should have known better. Then Eve looked up at him, her bright-blue eyes luminous with happiness, and he didn't care. She felt good in his arms—warm and curvy and...right. If holding her close meant he had to work to keep from becoming too aroused, then so be it.

The music went sweet, then sad, full of melancholy. For Damien, the music barely registered, other than a beat to which to move his feet. Eve Kelley, melting in his arms, was as close to heaven as he'd ever been.

The song finished and rather than launching into another, Ian, the lead singer, announced they were taking a ten-minute break.

Heart pounding, Damien led Eve off the dance floor and back to their booth. He couldn't believe how strongly she affected him. Obviously, he didn't have the same effect on her.

"That was nice," she smiled up at him. "I haven't had this much fun in a long time. "

"Take your hands off her," a male voice shouted.

They both turned. Ian Murphy. Fists clenched, complexion mottled, the other man looked ready to fight.

Still pressed close into Damien's side, Eve groaned. "Cut it out, Ian."

Instead, Ian moved closer, his mouth twisted with disapproval. "What are you doing with him? For Chrissake, Eve. He's an ex-con! I've only been back in town a few days, but even I've heard about him."

At the other man's words, Damien took a step forward. Eve's gentle squeeze on his arm stopped him.

"He was wrongfully convicted, Ian." To Damien's disbelief, she moved even closer to him, as if she wanted to meld into his side. "And who I date is absolutely none of your business."

Ian's fair complexion turned a violent shade of red, but instead of arguing or, worse, picking a fight he'd surely lose, he spun around and stormed off.

Damien would have welcomed the fight, though it wouldn't have helped his status around Honey Creek.

Next to him, he felt Eve relax. "I think I'd better leave."

"Old flame?" he asked, keeping his tone light.

"Really old. We dated before he went off to Nashville and made it big. That was eighteen months ago."

Back at their table, she gathered her purse and coat. "I'm sorry, Damien. I'd really better go."

Unable to help himself, he caught her arm. "Let me go with you."

As she peered up at him, her pupils dilated, and he caught his breath. Finally, she gave the slightest of nods. "Come on then."

He didn't wait to be asked twice.

On the way to the door, Eve had second thoughts. And again as she climbed in her truck. What on earth was she thinking? Half of the Corner Bar would have noted her and Damien leaving together. Worse, since he was following her home in his vehicle, if anyone drove past her house...

Stop it. Stop it right now. She was lonely, he was lonely. They wanted each other and were both adults. What would be the harm?

As long as Damien understood this could only be physical. No strings. Why borrow trouble when she already had enough of her own?

Snow flurries drifted in her headlights as she drove home. Aware her car heater wouldn't even kick on until she was nearly home, Eve shivered as she tried to stay warm.

Hitting the automatic garage-door opener, she pulled into her garage and parked, wondering yet again if she wasn't making a horrible mistake.

Yet, thinking of how she'd felt dancing close to Damien brought a rush of warmth, and she reminded herself she didn't care.

Damien Colton was addicting. Something about him... She'd given in to that craving sixteen years ago and now that he'd returned, she was beginning to think she hadn't ever gotten him out of her system.

Damien parked in the driveway behind her, his extended-cab pickup too large to fit in her garage. Heart in her throat, she watched him stride toward her. When he reached her, he didn't speak, but instead gathered her close and kissed her. Right there in her garage, both of them still bundled in parkas, his mouth covered hers with a hungry intensity that told her she wasn't alone in the fierceness of her need.

The feel of him, so big and male, made her shiver. As his lips blazed over hers, desire, raw and hot and heavy, banished all rational thought.

She wanted this man. Now.

Raising his mouth from hers, he gazed deeply into her eyes. "Are you sure?" he asked.

For one confused moment, she wondered if she'd spoken her thoughts out loud. Then she looked up at him and her heart lurched. Despite his apparent confidence, she sensed his vulnerability.

Instead of answering his question with words, she wound her arms inside his jacket and raised up to touch her mouth to his, giving him her answer with her body instead.

It was like kindling erupting into flame. Her body tingled, burned as she wrapped herself around him, yearning to be closer still.

Somehow, still kissing, they stumbled toward the door.

Though they were still wound around each other, she had the presence of mind to hit the close button for the garage door. As she did, she muttered a quick prayer that her mother wouldn't see Damien's truck parked in her driveway. Not that Bonnie Gene would mind, but a full-out interrogation would be sure to follow.

Then, as his mouth grazed her ear and burned a path down her cheek and neck, she forgot about everything else but the magnificent man in her arms.

They made it inside, though she didn't know how. She came up for air long enough to realize they were in her bedroom.

Shedding her coat, she let it fall at her feet, watching as he did the same.

"Come here."

Throat tight, she moved closer to him, aching for him to caress her.

Instead, he began to remove her sweater, helping her tug her arms free. He undressed her slowly, gazing at her with a burning intensity, as if memorizing her with his eyes.

Finally naked while he stood still fully clothed, she squirmed against him, seeking to taunt him into losing control. From the harsh intake of his breath, she'd succeeded, but still he didn't move.

"Easy now," he told her, his voice sounding like smoke and gravel, a contrast with the cool brush of his hands against her skin. "Patience."

She tried to hold back, trembling with both cold and need, but with her desire mounting, she simply could not. With a curse of frustration she tore at his clothes, impatient to see him, to rake her nails against his rock-hard abs and explore his muscular body with her fingers.

Lifting his hands, he let her undress him, the heat in his gaze promising all sort of pleasure when she'd finished. As she fumbled with his belt buckle, he helped her, and when she unbuttoned his jeans, and freed him, he made a sound of pleasure low in his throat.

Holding back her wildness, she caressed the hard length of him, marveling at the thickness and size of his erection, wickedly amused as he froze, as if afraid to move.

Then, grabbing her hands to stop her, he pulled her hard up against him, flesh to flesh, man to woman.

"I don't have a condom," he rasped. "I had a complete physical when I got out, and I'm still clean, but... Sorry, but I wasn't expecting..."

"It's okay." Her chest hurt from wanting him so badly. "I'm already pregnant. And they tested me for everything when I had the pregnancy confirmed, so we ought to be all right."

Fire in his gaze, he slanted his mouth over hers, both demanding and giving. Fire and ice, summer and winter, trembling with passion, they fell onto the bed. She sighed as she found herself underneath him, his aroused sex hard and heavy against her thigh.

Arching her back, she gasped as his mouth closed over her nipple, shuddering as he touched her, skimming the curve of her waist, stroking her moistness.

She cried out as he entered her, filling her.

"Perfect," he murmured, his lips curving as he began to slowly move.

As he did, the ache sparked by his kiss exploded into flame. Her body throbbed as he entered her completely and then withdrew, leaving her aching for him. Waves of passionate ecstasy filled her as they moved together, body-to-body, so close she couldn't tell where she ended and he began.

Her passion became mindless. She cried out, and he answered her with a deep thrust.

Just like that, she shattered into a thousand pieces.

As she clenched around him, he groaned, sending waves of ecstasy into her core with each long, deep stroke. A moment later, he found his own release, crying out and collapsing against her.

They held each other, their bodies damp from lovemaking, sated. She liked that she felt so comfortable with him, liked that she didn't feel the need to fill the space with vague conversation.

When he rose to clean up, she watched him walk to her bathroom and admired the view from behind. He turned and caught her watching and grinned before closing the door behind him.

This just might work out, she congratulated herself as she lay back in her bed, hands behind her head. All her life she'd gone into relationships with high expectations. Now, having learned her lesson, she had no expectations at all. Why ask for more when she'd never gotten more? Less heartache, more pleasure. Good all the way around.

Now, if only she could make herself believe it.

And if her heart gave a twinge whenever she thought of Damien moving away, she put it down to the newness of things, nothing more.

She'd been a fool back in Italy. She wouldn't make that mistake again.

Chapter 8

Working at the salon was becoming more and more difficult, the further along Eve got in her pregnancy. Her back was killing her. If she felt this bad at only four months, she wondered what she'd be like at eight.

She watched Mrs. Grant, her eight-thirty shampoo and set, walk to her car. Luckily her next customer wasn't due for another fifteen minutes, so Eve could take a quick apple-juice break and rest her feet.

The changes that had begun to take place in her body both amazed and thrilled her. Not only had she began to 'ripen' as she thought of it, with fuller breasts and a softly rounded stomach, but her ankles now swelled when she stood on her feet all day. And the exhaustion! It seemed she barely had time to finish her breakfast and begin her workday and she craved a nap.

Like now. Stifling a yawn, she grabbed her juice from the fridge and dropped into her desk chair, unwrapping her midmorning granola bar.

The sleigh bells on the front door jingled merrily. Lacy Nguyen, her part-time stylist, waved at her as she came in. "Good morning," she sang out. "Sure smells like snow out there."

Eve laughed. "When does it not? It's December in Montana. If it didn't smell like snow, I'd be more surprised."

"Still, I'd love some Christmas snow. Maybe we could build a magical snowman!" Lacy grinned as she hung up her parka. "I've got a full day booked today."

"Good." Barely stifling a yawn, Eve took another bite of her granola bar. "I do, too."

Lacy studied her. "You look… Hey, are you seeing someone?"

Eve almost choked on her granola. "What? No. Why do you ask?"

"Because you're glowing." Lacy shrugged. "You know, like you're in love or something?"

Relieved, Eve laughed. If Lacy only knew. "Nope. The latest on the dating front is that I went on another disastrous blind date my mom set up. This time it was with that new attorney, Gary Jackson."

"Ewww." Lacy made a face. "He hit on me once. Didn't seem to mind when I said I was engaged."

The doorbells jingled again. Both women looked up, and froze. Maisie Colton stood in the doorway, wearing a bright-orange full-length down coat and fuchsia-and-orange striped scarf and gloves. Even with her windblown hair, she looked as though she'd just finished posing for a glossy magazine advertisement on winter.

"Eve?" She stepped inside, her high heels clicking on the linoleum. "Do you have a minute to talk?" Her gaze cut to Lacy. "Privately?" she added.

Immediately, Lacy snatched up a load of freshly washed

towels. "I'll be in the back, folding these," she said, darting a meaningful look at Eve. "If you need me, just yell."

"What can I do for you, Maisie?" Eve asked carefully.

"I wanted to talk to you about Gary Jackson. I know you were out with him the other night—"

Now Eve understood. Maisie was interested and wanted to make sure she wasn't encroaching on Eve's territory. What was up with that? Since when had Maisie cared?

"Gary and I were on a blind date set up by our mothers. I have absolutely no interest in him and I have no doubt he feels exactly the same way."

"Really?" Maisie's heart-shaped face lit up, making Eve realize exactly how beautiful Damien's sister was. "I wanted to make sure. He asked me out for next weekend."

Curious, Eve decided to be blunt. "Why do you care what I think?"

The question didn't seem to faze Maisie.

"I know it might seem weird. In the past, if I wanted something, I took it." Her perfectly painted lips curved. "I guess I just realized I had to grow up sometime. I'm trying to repair the damage I've done to people in this town."

"That's why you joined my mother's quilting group?"

"Yes. And I haven't actually joined yet. I'm still trying to get up the nerve to go to a meeting."

Really? Maisie Colton, frightened of something? "What are you afraid of?"

Taking a deep breath, Maisie met Eve's gaze, unsmiling. "Those other women don't like me much."

Eve didn't know what to say. Maisie had spoken the truth and to try and dilute that with platitudes or reassurance would only undermine it. Still, she had to say *something*.

"Do you know how to quilt?"

"No." Maisie brightened. "But your mother promised

to teach me. I want to make a quilt for my son, sort of an heirloom thing."

Touched, despite herself, Eve nodded. "And you came here because you want me to help you figure out how to get along with all those women?"

"No." Maisie Colton shook her head, sending her wayward hair flying. "I came here because I want you to cut my hair."

Then, while Eve was still reeling from this shocking news, Maisie made a scissoring motion with her fingers, right below her chin. "I want it cut short. Very short."

Still staring, Eve swallowed. "Seriously?"

"Yes, seriously." Stalking over to Eve's chair, Maisie sat. "Let's get busy. You've got to get me finished before your next client comes in."

True. Shaking out the vinyl cape, Eve draped it around Maisie's shoulders. "Let's get you shampooed."

Maisie's hair was thick and lustrous, much like her brother's. Eve shampooed and rinsed and wrapped her in a towel, before leading her back to the chair and combing her out. "Now tell me what kind of a haircut you want."

Maisie grinned. "I'll do better. I'll show you." She grabbed her purse, rummaging inside and finally pulling out a folded square that had obviously been taken from a magazine. "Here you go. It's Rihanna. A pixie crop with a sweeping fringe."

"So it is." Eve glanced from the picture to Maisie. "You do realize this will involve me cutting off at least six inches?"

"Sure."

Relentlessly determined, Eve continued. "And you'll have to use styling products and a flat iron after you blow-dry?"

"I already do. Let's go for it."

"Fine." Eve grabbed her scissors and began. She couldn't help but wince as the long locks fell to the floor. "Does your brother know you're doing this?"

"Which brother?"

"Any of them," Eve said, refining her cut around the back. "Wes, Finn, Brand, Perry, Duke or Damien."

"No. But then I'm not in the habit of consulting my brothers before I get a new haircut." Taking a deep breath, Maisie closed her eyes. "He was with you last night, wasn't he?"

Eve was so busy snipping away that Maisie's words barely registered. "Who?"

"My brother. Damien."

Eve nearly cut off a huge swath of Maisie's silky hair. Accidentally, of course. "Ummm, maybe," she said hesitantly. "Why?"

Maisie opened her eyes. "I just want to know what your intentions are toward him."

Dumbfounded, Eve met the other woman's gaze in the mirror. "My intentions?"

"Yes. Damien's fragile. He doesn't really know how to react to the regular world. He's only been out a few months."

"Fragile. Huh." Resuming cutting, Eve couldn't seem to get past repeating parts of Maisie's words. "I think you should ask him."

"I tried." Pouting, Maisie sounded disgruntled. "He told me what he did in his spare time was none of my business."

Relieved, Eve began to shape the hair at the side of Maisie's face. "He's right, you know."

"Maybe. But someone has to look out for him. No one else will, so it might as well be me."

This struck Eve as both touching and funny, for some

reason. The image of Damien hiding behind his slender and glamorous sister made her want to laugh. Her mouth twitched, but she succeeded in holding it in.

Almost.

"Don't laugh," Maisie complained. "I'm serious."

"I understand." Brandishing her scissors high, Eve smiled. "Did it ever occur to you not to shock the woman who's cutting your hair?"

Maisie's perfectly made-up eyes widened. "You wouldn't," she breathed.

"No, of course not. I was just trying to get you to lighten up." She shook her head. "I'm a professional. Plus, I'd like you to come back. I know if I do a good job, you might."

Finally, Maisie's shoulders relaxed. "I *was* tense, wasn't I? I'm sorry. I try so hard, but I've never really gotten along with other women."

That was the understatement of the year.

The jingle bells signaled the arrival of Lacy's client. Emerging from the back room, Lacy did a double take to see Eve cutting Maisie Colton's hair. Eve shot her a warning look and the other stylist went to collect her customer, who also stared hard at Maisie. The news that Maisie Colton had gotten her hair cut at Eve's Salon Allegra would be all over town before the end of the day.

Finishing the cut, Eve sprayed Maisie's hair with a root booster and began blow-drying, showing the other woman how to style with a roller brush, then using a flat iron.

When she'd finished, she stepped back to survey the results before turning Maisie around to face the mirror.

"This might just be the perfect haircut for you," she said, letting Maisie see.

"Wow!" Maisie breathed, turning her head this way and that. "It looks really good." She shook her head, experimenting. "My head feels really light. I never realized how heavy all that hair was."

Removing the cape, Eve smiled. "I'm glad you like it."

After Maisie had paid and left, Eve checked her watch. Mrs. Peterson, her next customer, was late. As she was walking to check her appointment desk, the phone rang. It was Mrs. Peterson, canceling. Which meant Eve had an entire hour before Damien was due to arrive for his haircut. She went in the back to put her feet up and, she hoped, take a catnap.

She'd actually dozed off when the sound of the bells woke her. Peeking out front, she saw that Lacy's client had left. And the second she did, Lacy hurried back and plopped down into the chair next to Eve. "Tell me, tell me everything."

Covering her mouth while she yawned, Eve found herself feeling oddly defensive on Maisie's behalf. "Tell you what? There's nothing to tell. She wanted a haircut. I gave her one. That's what I'm in business for, right?"

Lacy looked unconvinced. "Well, yeah. But Maisie Colton never stoops to having her hair cut here. You know as well as I do that she always goes to Billings. We're not sophisticated enough for her."

"Maisie Colton is trying to change."

Lacy opened her mouth to argue when the bells jingled again.

Glancing at the clock, Eve stood. "My next client." She wondered if she should warn Lacy, then decided not to. It would be fun to see her face.

"Mine should be here any minute, too." Lacy would surely get her second shock of the day.

* * *

Usually having sex put Damien in a good mood, freed his pent-up tension and relaxed him. Not this time. The entire weekend, he'd been tense and restless, unable to stop thinking about Friday night and making love with Eve. Already he'd wanted her again; he'd reached for her first thing when he woke on Saturday morning. He'd never done that before and it worried him.

The rest of the weekend hadn't been any better. He'd wanted her at odd moments during the day. In fact, he'd had to force himself not to go to the Corner Bar on Saturday night, not wanting Eve to think he needed more than she was willing to give.

Evidently he hadn't gotten her out of his system yet.

Sunday and Monday had both been much of the same. He'd kept himself busy, rising at the crack of dawn and saddling up to ride out in the early-morning chill. He and his gelding had slogged through snow, keeping an eye out for any straggling cattle, and watching the sun come up over the mountains.

Days like these made him wonder how he could ever leave Montana or this ranch. The land was in his blood, as vital to him as fresh air. Sometimes he thought if he had the land, a horse and a few hundred head of cattle, he wouldn't need anything else.

Except sex, he amended. Again, he thought of Eve and shifted in the saddle. She could easily become an addiction. He craved her, craved the feel and scent of her, the satiny smoothness of her skin.

Again, he was struck by a sharp sense of need. Eve. No, he told himself. It didn't have to be her. Any woman would fit the bill. He wanted more sex. Lots of it, plain and simple. Not Eve.

But he knew he was only lying to himself.

Damn it to hell. She'd done something to him. Usually, the physical release after sex lasted him at least a week, sometimes longer if he kept busy.

But not this time. After making love with Eve, all he could think about was being with her again. He felt as if he'd been literally starving and she'd been a feast. A feast he couldn't get enough of.

He had to stay away, prove he could tough this out.

Still, he was glad he'd made the hair appointment with her for today. He needed a haircut and that would be a perfect time to prove he was immune to her lure.

After performing his morning chores, he'd plowed through lunch. All day he'd had an eagerness lurking low in his gut.

When it had come time to drive to town, he'd felt unaccountably nervous and edgy. He, who had faced down a three-hundred-and-sixty-pound enraged, territorial prison inmate, dreaded facing slender Eve Kelley. As if she could simply take one look at him and know he'd spent the last fifty-six hours thinking about her.

The walk from his truck to her salon door seemed far too long. Boots crunching in the frozen snow, he reached the door, wondering for the eightieth time why he hadn't just gone to the Old Time Barber Shop like he, and all the other Colton men, always did.

But he knew the answer to that. He wanted to see Eve.

Little bells jingled as he yanked open the door to Salon Allegra. Approaching the front counter, he saw the shop was empty and breathed a sigh of relief. The last thing he needed was to have a bunch of women with foil or curlers in their hair staring at him.

Then Eve emerged from the back, her smile so warm, so welcoming, he felt he could face down an entire army of gossiping women. He barely noticed a second woman following Eve, then stopping in her tracks and staring at him, openmouthed.

"You made it!" Eve sounded glad—and surprised.

Nodding, he smiled, managing to keep the smile plastered on his face while she introduced the other woman, Lacy Nguyen.

Eve whisked a cloak around him. "Follow me. We'll get you shampooed, then you can tell me how you'd like me to cut your hair." She took him to the back, waited until he had taken a seat, then ran the water.

Spraying his head with warm water, she began to massage his scalp with shampoo. Her deft fingers felt so good, he nearly moaned. Instead, he closed his eyes.

Apparently as nervous as he, Eve kept up a constant monologue as she worked. "Poor Lacy doesn't know what to think. First your sister, then you—"

He snapped open his eyes. "My sister? Maisie came here?"

"Yes. She had me cut her hair really short. The cut she wanted wouldn't work on just anyone, but on her it's fabulous. Wait until you see her."

"I'm more interested in what she had to say."

Eve colored, a dead giveaway. Rinsing his hair off, she wrapped his head in a white towel, then began to do a quick towel-dry. For a moment, he thought she wouldn't answer. Then, she lifted one shoulder in a quick shrug.

"She asked me what my intentions were toward you."

He laughed. "What did you say?"

Glancing around to make sure Lacy couldn't hear, Eve leaned in close and whispered in his ear, "I told her they were purely sinful."

Shocked by both her words and the quick flick of her tongue on his ear, he froze.

Her laugh was more musical than the bells on her door.

"Really?" he managed. "I can just imagine Maisie's reaction."

"Just kidding," Eve continued merrily, as if oblivious to her effect on him. "In a roundabout way, I told her it was none of her business."

"Did she take that well?"

"Well, she didn't throw a temper tantrum or anything, so I guess so." She ran her fingers through his hair, testing texture and length. "Now tell me how you want this cut."

Fifteen short minutes later, eyeing himself in the mirror, Damien admitted she'd done a good job. She'd trimmed his unruly hair into a much neater do, managing to make his longish style look both hip and clean. "I won't be spraying any of that stuff on it after I shower," he warned her. "I usually just towel-dry and go."

Her blue eyes widened. "You go out into the subzero temperature with wet hair?"

"It dries long before I head out." He got out his wallet. "How much do I owe you?"

She waved him away. "Nothing. It's on the house."

An awful suspicion worried him. "Did you cut my sister's hair on the house also?"

Eve grinned. "Nope. I charged her thirty-five bucks."

"For a haircut?"

Her grin widened. "No need to sound so shocked. She pays twice that at the place she normally goes." She licked her lips, a mischievous twinkle in her eyes. "I'm worth it."

"Yes," he agreed, even as his body stirred. "You are." He got out two twenties and placed them on the counter. "Here you go."

"Men's cuts are only twenty." She slid one of the bills back toward him.

He slid it back. "Then this is your tip."

Coloring, she nodded. "Okay, then. Thanks."

Conscious of the other woman watching, he leaned closer. "Are you busy later on? I was thinking we could hang out tonight, if you want."

Again she flashed him a smile as her lashes swept down to cover her eyes. But only for a second, then she lifted her chin and her clear blue gaze met his.

"I'd like that," she said softly. "Where and when?"

"I'll pick you up at your place. Say, seven? We'll go grab a bite to eat."

"Why don't you bring food over instead?" she murmured, apparently also conscious of Lacy's inquisitive stare. "I don't think I'm going to feel much like going out."

Zing. Just like that, she had the capacity to stop his heart. "Okay," he managed. "What time?"

"Six is good. The earlier the better." Then, while he was still reeling from the possibilities in her smile, she walked away, waving goodbye at him over her shoulder.

He left the salon in a daze.

"Do you have a date?" Lacy followed Eve into the back room.

"No, of course not." Eve knew her denial came too quickly. Another dead giveaway would be the rush of color staining her cheeks.

"I swear I heard Damien Colton ask you out," Lacy persisted. "And I'm pretty sure you answered yes."

"First off, we're not going out." Truth, since they were staying in. "And secondly, Damien and I are just friends."

"Since when?"

"Since high school," Eve shot back, shooting her employee a look that plainly told her to back off. "Nothing to gossip about. Just two old friends catching up."

"Okay, have it your way." Clearly skeptical, Lacy shook her head. "But let me point out that if the two of you are such good friends, Damien's been home for months and this is the first time he's been in the shop."

Since Eve didn't have an answer for that one, she let it go. Time to change the subject and try to put things back on a normal footing.

"Speaking of the Coltons, today's turning out to be a Colton Monday," Eve said, finger on her appointment book. "First Maisie, then Damien and next Sharon, though she's the only one who actually had an appointment in advance."

Sharon Colton, Darius Colton's wife, was due in for her usual highlights and cut. She had a standing appointment once a month and was meticulous about keeping her frosted blond hair looking exactly the same. Though some found her standoffish, Eve liked the older woman, who had a lot to cope with in marrying into the Colton family as she had, especially since she was Darius's third or fourth wife. She rarely left the ranch, and when she came to town, it was either to get her hair or nails done, or to eat at Eve's family's famous barbecue restaurant.

Even the Coltons were unable to resist the perfection of the Kelley's slow-cooked brisket or smoked ribs. The restaurant was especially busy this time of the year with its smoked holiday turkeys.

"Better you than me," Lacy said, yawning and apparently giving up. "This has been a long day. I'm ready to call it a day."

"Me, too. I just have this one more customer, then I can lock the place up and head home."

The bells over the front door tinkled, telling them Sharon had arrived. Hurrying out into the salon area, Eve stopped short at her first glimpse of her client. Usually,

Sharon Colton looked like a less dramatic version of Maisie—perfectly put together, remote and fashionable. Not today.

Though she wore one of the many full-length fur coats her rich cattleman husband had given her, her heart-shaped face looked drawn and pale. The huge circles under her blue eyes made her look tired, and every tiny line stood out in stark relief. Many of the townspeople believed she went to Bozeman on a regular basis and got Botox treatments, but looking at her this morning, Eve doubted it.

"Are you all right?" she asked softly.

Sharon looked up, swaying slightly. "I think so. Or I will be, once I finish getting pampered." Her tight smile didn't reach her eyes. As usual she spoke with a hint of a Southern accent, the kind that blurred her words and softened consonants.

If she didn't want to elaborate, Eve wouldn't make her. "Well, come on then." Eve patted her chair. "Have a seat and let me mix up your color. I won't be a minute."

Sharon complied, sitting quiet and stiff while Eve draped a cloak around her. Eve left her there, going into the back room to prepare the color, returning with the mixture and her box of precut foils. They'd do the highlights first, as usual, then shampoo, color and style.

Sometimes Sharon chattered away, sometimes not. Today appeared to be one of the latter times, since Sharon closed her eyes while Eve began painting on the highlights, then wrapping them in foil. Because of her pregnancy, Eve wore two layers of rubber gloves and a mask to protect her, not wanting to take a chance. To her shock and amazement, Sharon fell asleep, dozing while Eve completed the highlights.

When she'd finished, she gently touched Sharon's slender

shoulder, waking her. "All right, it's time to go under the dryer."

"Give me a minute." The older woman blinked, speaking as though she were drugged.

"Are you sure you're okay?"

"Yes. No. Something's wrong at home," Sharon confessed abruptly, the anguish in her eyes wrenching Eve's heart. "Darius has been worse since Damien came home. I don't know what to do."

She actually sounded afraid. Even terrified. Then, before Eve could comment, she continued.

"I think my own husband is trying to kill me."

Chapter 9

"Trying to kill you?" Eve repeated, shooting Sharon a shocked look. "Why do you say that?"

As if she regretted saying anything, Sharon's expression shut down. Carefully blank, she shook her head. "Forget I said anything, all right?"

As if. Still, what else could Eve do?

Carefully considering her words, Eve slowly nodded. "If you need help, or just someone to talk to, call me. I'll write my cell phone number on the back of my card, all right?"

Instead of answering, Sharon looked away, her remote expression indicating the conversation was over. Eve led her to the dryer and left her, setting the timer for fifteen minutes.

In the back of the salon, Lacy had just finished removing the last load of towels from the dryer and folding them.

She looked up as Eve approached, then hurried over to take Eve's arm.

"Are you all right? You look awfully pale."

"I'm..." Eve had to think for a moment. "I'm fine. Just tired. I've got Sharon Colton under the dryer. After I finish with her, I'm going home."

Lacy studied her. "I was going to leave, but I'm thinking I'd better hang around in case you faint or something. Maybe you should sit down." She pulled out a chair.

Without even arguing, Eve sat. "Ah," she breathed. "That's better."

"Maybe you've been working too hard." Still concerned, Lacy fluttered around her like a mother hen. "You should consider taking a day off."

Eve waved her off. "I haven't been working too hard and I'll have plenty of time off for the Christmas holiday. Today's just been a rough one."

"I guess, with all the Coltons coming in and all." Finally, Lacy moved away. "Then if you really are all right..."

"You can go home. I've still got to rinse Sharon Colton, then cut and style her hair. I should be thirty more minutes tops."

Lacy eyed her slyly. "And then you can get ready for your big date with Damien Colton."

"It's not a date," Eve began automatically, stopping as Lacy burst into laughter.

"Call it whatever you want. Just have a nice night." Still giggling, Lacy waved as she headed toward the door. "See you tomorrow."

As she finished up with Sharon, Eve remained quiet, hoping to give the older woman a chance to talk if she wanted to. But Sharon said nothing else, her closed-off expression indicating she wasn't open to questions.

When Eve finished styling her hair, Sharon laid a crisp, one-hundred-dollar bill on the counter as she always did.

"Merry Christmas," she said, her attempt to appear carefree falling short. Swirling her fur coat around her shoulders, she sailed off.

Locking the door behind her, Eve wondered about Sharon's earlier remark. Surely she hadn't been serious, though her fear had seemed real enough.

Still, her own husband? Darius had been married three or four times, but all the marriages except the first one, the one who'd been the mother of most of the Colton children, had ended in divorce. Had Darius threatened Sharon? Was he abusive?

The answer to that, Eve didn't know. No one except his own family and maybe his business associates truly knew Darius Colton. Reclusive and secretive, the man seldom left the ranch. She'd heard gossip, but she didn't know what to believe about him, negative or otherwise. Maybe she should ask Damien.

Or, she told herself, shaking her head, maybe she should keep her nose out of other people's business.

Still, the fear in Sharon's eyes haunted her as she drove home.

Though he had a few more end-of-the-day chores to finish before he could clean up and head over to Eve's place, Damien couldn't concentrate on any of them. He felt like a teenager about to go on a date with the most popular girl in school.

Despite an outdoor temperature in the low twenties, he took a cold shower, trying to control his unruly body.

Then he had to decide on food. Honey Creek wasn't big enough to have a huge selection of fast-food places. Besides Kelley's Cookhouse and the Corner Bar and Grill, there was a pizza parlor, a hamburger joint and the newest place, a Mexican cantina. Guadalupe Torres and his wife, Angelina, had moved to Montana from Laredo, Texas, and wanted to introduce Mexican food to Honey Creek. Damien hadn't tried it yet and he was willing to bet neither had Eve.

Perfect. He phoned in an order for beef and chicken fajitas. He'd pick them up on the way to Eve's.

The drive from the ranch back into town went quickly, though it seemed agonizingly slow to him. But the food was ready and before he knew it, he was on his way.

The spicy aroma filled his car, making him realize he was hungry. This, oddly enough, relaxed him. Grinning as he pulled into Eve's driveway and parked, he grabbed the box of food and went to her front door.

He'd barely pressed the doorbell when she opened the door, wearing a red silky bathrobe. As she stepped back to let him enter, she closed the door behind her and took the food out of his hands, carrying it to the kitchen.

Not sure what to do, Damien waited in the living room, taking in her Christmas decorations. A fire roared in the stone fireplace and a slender Christmas tree stood in one corner, decorated in red, gold and green. He liked the simple, uncluttered look of the room, so different from his own family's all-out Christmas attack.

Behind him, Eve made a sound. When he turned, she strolled over to him, expression determined, and then, gaze locked with his, she stepped out of the robe.

Slipping her sleeves from her robe felt like one of the most daring things Eve had ever done. Heart pounding in her throat, she trembled as she lifted her chin and met Damien's glorious brown eyes. Then, taking a deep breath, she stepped out of her clothing, feeling way out of her comfort zone baring herself to him. She felt naked in more than her body—she felt naked in spirit, too.

She needn't have worried. Damien inhaled, a harsh sound, then his gaze darkened and he pulled her into his arms.

This time when they made love, she couldn't believe the way they immediately found an exquisite rhythm, a mutual harmony that made each kiss, every caress magic.

Now that the first rush of heady desire had become a steady, pulsing thrum, they were able to take their time exploring each other's bodies. She let herself luxuriate in the feel of him, gliding her hand over his muscular abdomen, caressing his broad shoulders and perfect abs. She delighted in teasing him, bending over him to take his nipples in her mouth, trailing kisses down the hard length of him until he shuddered and told her no more.

"My turn," he rasped, and nearly turned the tables. His lips traced a sensual path down her throat, to her breasts, and she let out a soft moan as he took her in his mouth.

Now she couldn't go slowly any longer. With fierce cries she urged him on. He shook his head and continued his teasing torture, until she'd finally had enough.

Pushing him over on his back, she straddled him. Poising herself over the hard length of his body, she lowered herself onto him, taking him deep within her and riding him until he bucked like a rodeo bronco.

Seconds later she found her release and as she did, he cried out and did the same.

Later, she microwaved the now-cold food and they feasted on fajitas. Covered by only a blanket, they sat on the rug near her fireplace and cuddled.

"How's Sharon doing?" she asked without thinking.

"I don't know. We hardly ever see her. She and Darius

have an entire wing to themselves and she keeps mostly to herself. Why?"

She knew he felt her tense. "No reason," she lied. "I cut her hair this afternoon and she wasn't feeling too well."

"Hmmm." He nuzzled her neck. "I'm sorry to hear that."

Though she knew she should let it go, she couldn't. "Sharon was worried about Darius. She thought he might... be angry at her."

Now he drew back. "There's more that you're not telling me, isn't there?"

Miserable, she nodded, then blurted out the whole story.

Damien listened, his expression thoughtful. "Please don't tell anyone else what you've told me."

"I won't," she hastened to reassure him. "But poor Sharon seemed so terrified, so I thought I'd better let you know so you could keep an eye on things."

"I will, believe me." Once again Damien pulled her close, holding her. The way he held her made her feel as though she was the most precious thing in the world. For half a second, before she took herself to task.

She was done wearing rose-colored glasses and she no longer believed in fairy tales or happy endings. It was time to call a spade and spade and be grateful for what she did have.

"About our arrangement..." Nervously, she pushed out of his arms and cleared her throat. "I think we should have some ground rules."

One corner of his mouth quirked in the beginning of a smile. "Okay. Shoot."

"First off, this is for fun. The minute it stops being fun for either of us, we can call it off, no hard feelings."

He nodded.

"Two, no emotional entanglements. Three, once I start showing, you can't make fat jokes. That is, assuming you still want to continue seeing me once I'm showing."

Now he did laugh. "Come here."

More afraid than she'd realized, she allowed him to pull her close once more. As he nuzzled her neck again, she found thinking difficult.

"You worry too much. One day at a time, Eve Kelley. One day at a time."

Then he covered her mouth with his and she gave up trying to think.

Back at the ranch after spending a few wonderful hours with Eve, Damien enjoyed a perfect night's sleep for the first time in ages. He awoke on Tuesday morning sated and refreshed and craving coffee.

Later, as he sipped his coffee and had to stop himself from whistling out loud, he realized that the world couldn't have gone completely crazy. If he tried really hard, he could just about convince himself that the two episodes with Darius were the result of his father being out of sorts due to having had a bad day and/or drinking too much.

Darius had long been the patriarch of the Colton clan, and was a well-respected rancher. He'd try talking to his father again. Surely, this time Darius would be more reasonable.

Even if he wasn't, Damien had no choice but to confront him. He had to find out where his money had gone. Darius owed him that much. If he couldn't replace the inheritance, he needed at least to provide a reasonable explanation for its disappearance.

He knew he could catch Darius in his office at this time of morning, attending to ranch business. Prudently, he gave the older man time to ingest a few cups of coffee, not sure if morning crankiness might be another of his sire's recent bad traits.

At least this time he'd be sober.

Tapping on the heavy oak door, Damien waited until Darius looked up from his paperwork. "Do you have a minute?"

Darius frowned, but he motioned to the chair in front of his desk. "What do you want?"

The rude question made Damien feel like a panhandler, let in from the cold and begging for a handout, but he forced himself to let the feeling slide away.

"I wanted to talk to you about my inheritance."

Immediately, Darius's expression twisted with anger. "That again. I've already told you, the money is gone. Live with it and quit bothering me."

"Last time we spoke, you'd had a few drinks." Damien kept his tone level, even soothing. "I understand the money is gone. What I'd like to know is where it went."

With a snarl, Darius removed his glasses and threw them onto the desk. "That is none of your business."

Damien felt as if the bell had just rung for round two. Why did all dealings with his father have to disintegrate into arguments and fights?

Taking a deep breath, Damien tried to tamp back his instinctive reaction to his father's behavior—his own anger. Maybe if he refused to let the old man goad him, they could eventually have a civil conversation.

Maybe.

"This *is* my business," he insisted. "It was my money and I'd like to know what you've done with it."

To his surprise, Darius actually nodded.

"Fair enough." Darius's expression smoothed over and his tone became pleasant. "As conservator, I invested it for you, hoping to make more money. As you know, the stock market tanked. I lost it. Every single penny."

Finally. A reasonable explanation.

"I'd like to see the transaction records."

Darius's expression hardened and his mouth thinned in displeasure, though his tone remained civil. "When I have time, I'll locate those and get them to you."

And now Damien had a choice. He could agree, aware Darius was putting him off and had no real intention of finding anything, or he could insist on seeing the records now. While the latter would be the most productive, it also was the most likely to provoke Darius into a rage.

Still, Damien hadn't come this far to back down now. Maybe if he kept everything calm and rational, Darius would follow his lead.

"Actually, I'd like to see them now."

"Actually," Darius mocked him. "That's not possible. I don't know where they are."

Now came the tricky part. "This is your office. I'm sure you must have a file for your stock transactions. If you'll let me review the file, I can make copies of anything pertaining to my money."

A flicker of horror flashed across the older man's face. "No. I'm too busy to deal with this right now. Plus, no one makes copies of my personal financial records. No one. Understand? Now go away."

Damien didn't move. "I'm not going anywhere. I'm well within my rights to ask to see records of my own money."

"You have no rights," Darius spat, his gaze full of contempt. "Now get out."

"Don't start this—"

"You started it by coming in here and demanding, in my own office, in my own house. How dare you demand anything from me. You ought to be grateful I give you a roof over your head, boy."

Face a glowering mask of rage, Darius stood and pointed toward the door. "Go away before I say something I might regret."

"What, you haven't already?" Damien didn't bother to hide his disappointment. "All this shadow-dancing makes me think you really do have something to hide."

"You don't even know the half of it," Darius sneered. "I could snap my fingers and have you killed, just like that."

This stopped Damien cold. "What are you saying?"

"I'm just saying, don't go poking your nose in places it doesn't belong, understand me?"

"You're my father." Damien felt as if a heavy weight pressed against his chest. "How can you talk like that to me?"

In reply, Darius gave a nasty chuckle. "I can't allow personal relationships to get in the way of business. This is business. I told you to leave before you heard something you didn't want to hear. The truth isn't always pretty, now, is it?"

"I wonder if you even know what the truth really is." Finally, realizing that if he wanted answers, he'd have to get them on his own, Damien pushed to his feet. "I just hope that when I find out what really happened, I don't discover you have been lying to me."

"Or what?" Darius crossed his arms, his face hard. "You gonna treat me like some of your prison buddies no doubt treated you?"

Instead of dignifying this awful statement with a response, Damien slammed out of the room, Darius's mocking laughter following him, making him want to hit something.

In the kitchen, he grabbed the wall phone and dialed the sheriff's office. Wes answered on the second ring.

"I'm calling a family meeting," Damien announced.

Wes cursed. "Not now. I don't have time for this."

"Make time. Things are worse here than you realize."

"You don't understand. I'm working a murder investigation."

Damien didn't pull any punches. "You'll be working another one if we don't deal with Darius now."

Shocked silence. Then, as Damien had known he would, Wes agreed to be there.

Finn was easier. "Sure," he agreed. "As long as it's at night or on a weekend, I'll drive out to the ranch."

"Tonight, seven o'clock."

"That soon? Things must really be bad. Okay, count me in. I'll be there."

Two down, five to go. Next, Damien phoned Duke.

"Tonight, Susan wants me to help her pick out food for the wedding." Duke sounded as though he'd rather wallow in pig excrement. "If I tell her I have an emergency family meeting, I think I can get out of it."

"I'll need you to back me up on what's been going on around here."

"Can do." Sounding relieved, Duke hung up to go find his fiancée and tell her the news.

Last, Damien went looking for Maisie. He'd been surprised when Eve had told him she'd cut his sister's hair. Last he'd heard, Maisie had been paying over a hundred bucks for a haircut at some fancy salon up in Billings.

When she opened the door after his knock, and he saw her, he was shocked speechless.

"You like it?" She preened, spinning around so he could get the full effect. "Eve did a wonderful job."

"Wow! When she said she'd cut your hair, I had no idea,"

he began. The look of glee in his sister's eyes made him realize his mistake.

"You saw her?"

He crossed his arms. "Yes. Yesterday. She cut my hair, too. Why?"

"She didn't say anything about seeing you. I even asked her about her intentions."

"You did what?"

"Asked her about your intentions. When did you get your hair cut?"

"After you." Swearing under his breath, he shook his head. "I already told you, none of your business." He shook off his irritation. This was Maisie, after all. She'd always danced to the beat of her own drum. "We're having a family meeting at seven tonight. Perry, Joan and Brand aren't around, and you and Jeremy need to be in attendance, all right?"

She nodded, then looked dubious. "Is Darius going to be there?"

"No. Darius is the reason we're having a meeting. We're going to discuss him."

"Behind his back?" Maisie scrunched up her nose. "He won't like that."

"He's not going to find out. Just be there, Maisie. Okay?"

Finally, she agreed. "Make sure you have something to eat. I'm usually hungry around seven," she said. Then, claiming she needed a nap, she closed the door in his face.

That evening, waiting in the kitchen as everyone straggled in, Damien tried to plan what he wanted to say. The others had to understand that Darius was ill and apparently had been for quite some time.

Maisie arrived last, after the others were seated. Since

he'd called the meeting, Damien remained standing. Pacing helped him articulate better.

Damien cleared his throat. When everyone had fallen silent, he began. He told them about the disappearance of his inheritance, then recounted the scene with Darius in his office that morning.

"He threatened to kill you?" Duke's tone reflected his shock.

Even Maisie appeared stunned. Only Jeremy gave no reaction, but continued stuffing his face with gingerbread cookies.

"Yes. He intimated that he could have someone do the deed. Like he'd done it before."

"Now wait a minute," Wes pushed to his feet. "This is crazy. Darius may be a lot of things, but he's still our father. I know he's been growing increasingly unstable, but murder—whether for hire or otherwise—is a serious crime. Darius knows that. He won't risk the ranch and our futures, not to mention his own, for something like that."

"I don't think Darius gives a rat's ass about any of us," Damien said. "And as for risking the ranch, I believe he already has."

Finn shook his head. "You have no proof. You're saying that based on what happened with your inheritance."

"That, and the fact that he won't let me examine the books. Have any of you seen the books for this ranch?"

"No. Sharon does them for him. She used to be an accountant. Have you asked her?"

"No." Damien dragged his hand through his hair. "But I will, now that I know." He took a deep breath, meeting each of their eyes, one by one.

"Back to Darius. We need to get him in for medical tests. I think there might be something wrong. Either that or he's a sociopath." He attempted a chuckle, failing miserably.

"Finn, since you're the doctor in the family, you should handle that."

Finn gave an inelegant and decided un-doctorlike snort. "Just how do you propose I do that? Even if there is something wrong with him, which is a distinct possibility, he's a sixty-year-old adult man. I can't force him to submit to medical tests."

"You know Darius," Wes added. "He'll tell you to go to hell. I don't see how we can convince him to get help."

Duke spoke up. "Maybe Maisie can. She seems to have more sway with him than anyone else."

Before he'd even finished talking, Maisie shook her head. "He just views women differently, that's all. We're—me, Joan and Sharon, that is—his possessions. Objects in a way, not real people. If you think for a minute that he would allow me to try to tell him what to do..." She shuddered. "Not going to happen. I don't want to be the next one he comes at with a fireplace poker. No, thank you."

Jeremy lifted his head and swallowed the last bite of his cookie. "I think we should just leave Darius alone. He doesn't like any of us anyways. Maybe we could all move to a new ranch with Uncle Damien."

As one, they all turned to look at Damien.

"Move to a new ranch?" Finn frowned. "What's this all about, Damien? Why are you filling the kid's head with such nonsense?"

Even Maisie looked askance at him. "Honestly, you can't go around telling my son we're moving without even talking to me. You know I love Honey Creek. I'm not planning on going anywhere."

Before Damien could answer, Jeremy slammed the heel of his hand on the table. "That's typical, Mom. You do everything you can to ruin my life." He ran out of the room.

No one spoke as they watched him go. "Teenagers," Maisie said, to no one in particular. "What can you do?"

Finn steered the conversation back to Darius. "I'll talk to him, tell him it's time for him to have a physical. I'll run every test I can on him to make sure there's nothing wrong."

"Oh, there's definitely something wrong," Damien and Duke said at the same time. Sheepishly grinning at each other, they shrugged. As twins they finished each other's sentences all the time. Or had, until Damien had gone away to prison.

"What I'm trying to say," Finn continued, "is whatever is wrong with Darius may be mental rather than physical. If so, then nothing will show up on my test results."

"Even Alzheimer's?" Maisie asked.

"There is no test that can definitively diagnose Alzheimer's disease." Finn paused for a moment, thinking. "Though if I order a CT scan of his brain, it might be able to detect Alzheimer's plaques and tangles. It's all a crap shoot when it comes to that kind of stuff."

Still, it was the best they could do and they all knew it.

"There's more," Wes added slowly, sounding reluctant. "The Feds aren't in town just for the Mark Walsh murder. They're investigating Darius. It sounds pretty serious."

Chapter 10

"Investigating Darius? Why?" Duke asked. He, Finn and Maisie reacted with varying degrees of surprise and/or shock. Damien said nothing. How could he? The Feds had approached him days after he'd been released from prison. At the time, he'd thought they were crazy, so he'd readily agreed to help them. Now, he regretted that. The longer he was home and the more he tried to talk to Darius, the more he suspected the old man truly had something to hide.

"For what?" Finn sounded incredulous. "He's just a rich rancher. What could he possibly have done?"

"Besides stealing my inheritance?" Damien interjected dryly.

"You don't sound surprised," Wes said.

"I'm not, actually. The last I heard, they were looking at him for several things. Racketeering and money laundering being just two of them."

Wes narrowed his eyes. "You knew about this? How long have you known?"

With them all staring at him, Damien kept his face expressionless. "The Feds approached me right after I got out of prison. They wanted me to be their inside guy."

Wes swore. "They said they had someone on the inside. I didn't believe them." He cursed. "Especially you, of all people. The last person I would have suspected. Tell me, have you been reporting back to them?"

Crossing his arms, Damien studied each of his siblings. Their expression bore various degrees of surprise, shock or, in Maisie's case, disinterest. Still, the fact that Wes had to ask hurt. "I can't believe you asked that."

"Answer the question," Wes barked.

Pushing away a flash of anger, Damien shook his head.

"No, I haven't told the Feds a damn thing," he sighed.

"Why not?" Maisie interjected. "You know he's hiding something."

"Because I have nothing on him." Damien told the truth.

"Would you have told the Feds if you did?" Duke sounded merely curious, rather than condemning.

"I don't know. Personally, I think they should be kept out of this. Whatever he's done, I refuse to believe it's illegal. Darius might be acting crazy, but he's our father. We're all family here and all we have is each other. No matter what."

"I agree," Duke said. "Whatever he might be guilty of, it can't be that bad. This is family business and, bottom line, family is family."

Family is family. The Colton family's creed. Even if Darius himself appeared to have forgotten it, there was no reason any of them should betray him to the Feds.

Unless he actually hurt someone. That aspect needed to be addressed.

"That goes without saying," Wes seconded. "Unless of course, Darius does something completely crazy, like he's been threatening to do."

"Like kill me?" Damien asked. "Something has to be wrong with him. Something medical. I hope we get a handle on it before it gets to that point."

"We will." Duke sounded certain. "You've had a rough enough time of it already. It's a shame you're having to deal with this, too."

Damien silently agreed with that statement.

"I'll see if I can get him to agree to letting me do a complete physical. But for now, I've got to go." Finn glanced at his watch. "Rachel is waiting for me." The eagerness in his voice struck a chord of envy in Damien, making him wonder how it would feel to have a woman you loved waiting for you.

"Yeah, me, too." Wes walked to the door with his brother, turning when he reached the doorway. "We're all good, right? Medical tests from Finn and stonewall the Feds."

"Exactly," Damien answered. Still, Maisie said nothing, apparently engrossed in her nail polish.

The others all left, too, talking quietly among themselves.

Maisie said goodbye absently, picking at the polish on her index fingernail.

"Maise?" Damien moved closer. "What's wrong? You've been uncharacteristically quiet."

When she lifted her head to meet his gaze, her expression was troubled. "I think something really is wrong with Darius. You saw how he threatened to kill Sharon the other night."

"Like he did me."

"Yes." Maisie dragged her hand through her perfect hair, rumpling it. When she raised her gaze to meet his, fear shone in her eyes. "Damien, I think he really meant it. Sharon did, too. She looked absolutely terrified."

"I'll talk to her."

"No, don't." Maisie touched his arm. "I've already tried and she shut me out. I think she wants this to all just go away."

He sighed. "Don't we all."

"I know I do."

"Take it easy. Try to enjoy yourself. It's nearly Christmas. Do you have a date tonight?"

"Yes." For an instant her smile lit up her eyes, but then her face fell. "Only I'm not sure I want to see him anymore."

On alert, Damien watched her closely. "Has Gary Jackson done something to hurt you?"

"No, it's not that. It's just that he seems to have it in for you. He's really intense about it, Damien. He says he's assisting the Feds on an investigation concerning you. I'm worried they'll try to pin some crime Darius might have committed on you."

"Wouldn't that be par for the course?" He gave her a grim smile. "That's all I need. I've already been wrongly convicted of one crime."

Then, seeing how anxiety tightened her face, he tried to lighten the mood. "Come on, you know and I know that's not gonna happen. After all, what's the likelihood of lightning striking twice?"

"I don't know, but this still has me worried."

"Me, too." He thought for a moment. "I am kind of curious. Do you have any idea what Gary Jackson has against me, or why?"

She shrugged, avoiding his gaze. "I don't know."

Rising, she carefully placed her water glass in the

sink. Still not looking at him, she made a beeline for the hallway.

"Where are you going?" he asked, once again confused by her mercurial mood swings.

"To bed."

"I thought you had a date."

"I'm going to cancel it." Head held high, she sailed from the room, shooting him a look that dared him to follow.

He didn't. Though every bit of her demeanor suggested she was hiding something, Damien let her go. He was tired of drama, tired of secrets and hidden meanings. He longed to saddle up his gelding and take off for the open range, where only cattle and eagles would be his companions.

If it had been summertime, that's exactly what he would have done. Since it was winter and already dark, not to mention twelve degrees outside with the temperature falling fast, he did what he really wanted to do.

He got in his truck and headed over to Eve's. She was fast becoming an obsession with him. He dreamed about her at night, thought about her a hundred random times during the day. He ached to hold her, touch her, feel her lush body pressed up against him.

Though he desired her, Eve was special. He wanted more. More than just for sex, he wanted to be with her— after all, she was the closest thing he had to a friend.

The knock on her front door roused Eve from a deep sleep. She'd fallen asleep on the sofa again, with a Christmas special playing on the TV and her Christmas-tree lights twinkling in the background. Yawning, she rubbed her eyes and pushed to her feet, feeling ungainly and ungraceful, even though she'd only gained six pounds. Tightening the belt on her robe, she padded to the door and peeked through the peephole.

Damien. Snow dusting his cowboy hat, he looked good enough to eat. Beautiful and sexy, a wounded, lost man. Exactly the kind that always got her in trouble.

For no reason at all, her eyes filled with tears. Sniffing, she opened the door and let him in.

"What's wrong?" Sounding concerned, he pulled her close. He smelled of snow and leather, an outdoorsy, manly scent that embodied his essence.

"Nothing." She took a deep, shaky breath and wiped at her eyes. "Pregnancy hormones, I guess." Grabbing the old quilt she used to keep warm on the couch, she swung it over her shoulders and sat down.

"Were you asleep?" His deep voice rumbled with humor.

She glanced at the mantel clock before answering. "Maybe."

His grin warmed her more than any quilt. "Do you want me to leave?"

She punched him lightly in the arm. "I think you know the answer to that."

Taking off his cowboy hat, he hung it on her coatrack. As he removed his parka, he shot her a mischievous look. "Got any room under that blanket?"

Instead of answering with words, she lifted a corner of the quilt. Grinning, he came over and sat next to her, jeans-clad thigh next to her pajamas.

"You feel cold," she told him, snuggling against him. Then, as he lifted his hand to her cheek, she gasped. "Dang. Didn't you wear gloves?"

"No. I was in too big a rush to get here."

She searched his face. "Why? Did something happen?"

"I missed you, Eve." He kissed her. Taking his time,

letting the drowsy heat of her warm his cold lips. "I've really missed you today."

He sounded truly perplexed, which made her smile. Pleasure filled her for a moment, until she got a grip on herself and shook her head. No warm and fuzzy feelings here. Men said stuff like that all the time as a prelude to wanting sex. They didn't mean it. He didn't mean it either. She had to remember to take everything he said with a grain of salt. Otherwise, she'd end up hurt, with Damien running as far away as he could, leaving her alone with a broken heart.

Unfortunately, even thinking about doing without him made her feel weepy. "Damn hormones," she sniffed, while tears slowly tracked down her cheeks.

"Are you sure you're all right?" Big fingers gentle, he wiped the tears away.

"It's being pregnant," she explained, taking his hand and letting him feel the soft swell of her belly. "I'm a little past four months along now and the hormonal changes are making me act...different."

He nodded, his dark gaze finding hers. "Do you ever miss him?"

"Who?"

"The father of your baby. Massimo."

He remembered the name? She shook her head. "I barely knew him. I went to Italy because I was upset that I'm going to be forty soon. He was hot, we hit it off and the next thing I knew, we were in bed. He said all the right things, I wanted badly to believe him, and..." Lightly, she touched her belly. "Here I am. Hopefully wiser."

"When are you going to tell your family?"

"After New Year's. Since my sister and your brother are getting married on January second, I wanted to wait until that was over. Susan doesn't deserve me stealing her thunder."

"Ah, yes, the wedding." He pulled her closer. "I'm assuming you're a bridesmaid. I'm a groomsman. Wanna go together?"

For a second she couldn't breathe. "You mean...be each other's dates? In public?"

Now he watched her closely, his expression guarded. "Yes. Unless, of course, you're ashamed to be seen in public with me."

"Of course not. But I want you to consider this, Damien. Once I tell everyone that I'm pregnant, I'm not going to name the father."

"So?"

"Well, now you and I have an agreement not to get serious. But what if we ever started dating heavily, people might assume this is your baby." Grasping at straws, not even sure what was driving her.

A muscle worked in his jaw. Uncoiling himself from the couch, he stood. "I see. And for your child's sake, you don't think that's a good idea."

"It's just that..." Spreading her hands, she tried to find the right words to explain.

"Don't bother. You don't want people to assume your baby was sired by an ex-con. I get it. Don't bother getting up. I can find my own way out."

And he was gone.

Stunned, feeling as though she'd been hit by a ton of bricks, Eve huddled under her blanket, staring at the spot where he'd just been. What had all that been about? She'd only been trying to be practical, in keeping with their no-strings agreement. Damien was just out of sorts. Apparently she wasn't the only moody one in Honey Creek tonight.

* * *

Back home, insides churning, Damien parked next to an unfamiliar black sedan. Someone had company. Probably Maisie. After all, hadn't she mentioned she'd had a date with Gary Jackson tonight? Since she'd said she was going to cancel it, Gary had probably come to her.

His stomach rumbled, reminding him he hadn't eaten. He went to the kitchen and pulled out sandwich fixings. In the middle of making a sandwich, he heard the tap-tap-tap of Maisie's high heels headed his way.

"Hey, Maise." He greeted her as she strode across the ceramic tile. "Whose car is that in the driveway? Gary's?"

"No. Listen, there are a couple of men here to see you." Maisie looked worried. Moving closer, she said in a loud, stage whisper, "They say they're with the FBI."

Damien froze. The black car. "They're really pushing it, coming out here. Tell them to go away."

She shook her head, shooting him a weird look over her shoulder as she headed toward her room. "Tell them yourself. I put them in the study off the great room. That one guy scared me. He's built like an NFL linebacker."

Special Agent Donatello. It had to be. Maisie could charm most people and considered herself fearless. If someone frightened her... Donatello was a stereotypical law-enforcement official in love with his power. From his flat-top haircut and round spectacles, down to the long black trench coat he affected, he tried to appear a badass. In the entire time he'd been out of prison, Damien had never seen the man smile or crack a joke, and his humorless, no-nonsense attitude probably didn't win him any friends.

Damien had met Donatello when he'd first gone to talk to the Feds, willing to assist in the Mark Walsh investigation. Hell, he'd felt compelled to offer to assist in the investigation, and had been furious when they'd turned him away.

At the last second, they'd reconsidered and called him back. They did need his help on another investigation, they said. They were investigating his father. When Damien had demanded to know for what, they'd listed racketeering and money-laundering among a long list of other crimes.

Shocked, Damien had told them he'd help out. He'd gone home, regretting his words, and had managed thus far to avoid them.

Apparently, they'd gotten tired of waiting and had sent out the big guns.

Feeling as if he were heading to an execution—his own—Damien headed down the hallway toward the study. Two men, both wearing long black overcoats, waited with barely concealed impatience.

"What can I do for you gentlemen?" Damien asked.

Donatello swung his cold gaze around. "Why don't you tell us? You seem to have fallen off the grid."

The other agent, an older, gray-haired man, stepped forward. "What my colleague is trying to say is that we're close to finishing our investigation. We were expecting certain information from you. So far, you have not come forward with this information. Therefore, we are coming to you."

Seriously?

Aware he had to tread carefully, Damien manufactured a casual smile. "Could you be a little more specific? What information are you talking about?"

"Cut the crap, Colton," Donatello snarled. "You know what we mean." He took a step forward. "You agreed to help. We've done our part and stayed off your back. Now, unless you start producing, that will change."

"A threat is only effective when the person you're threatening understands what you're talking about," Damien felt obligated to point out. "Begin with explaining what you mean by 'stay off my back.'"

The two men exchanged a look. Then Donatello laughed. "We can put you under twenty-four-hour-a-day surveillance. Always watching, always waiting for you to make the slightest mistake. Do you want that?"

"Why me?" Damien spread his hands. "I'm not part of my father's financial dealings. I know nothing about them. His wife does the books, I think." Though he secretly doubted Sharon knew anything about his father's finances, he had no choice. "You might talk to her."

"Don't stonewall me." Donatello gave him a menacing look, which didn't bother Damien. After fifteen years in prison, he'd learned that looks alone couldn't hurt him. It's what came after the look that he had to worry about, and Donatello wouldn't touch him. Not here, not in front of witnesses.

"Look, I've been home since September." Damien smiled slowly. "I haven't seen anything out of the ordinary, so I have nothing to report to you." He put on a pained expression. "I don't understand why you can't comprehend that."

Though Donatello flushed beet-red, he knew there wasn't anything else he could do. "Come on," he told his partner. On the way out the door, he aimed one last parting shot at Damien. "We'll be back."

Damien couldn't resist one of his own. "Next time, you'd better have a search warrant."

Donatello slammed the door behind him.

As Damien walked to his room, Darius stepped in front of him, blocking his way.

"We need to talk," his father said, his commanding tone leaving no room for refusal. "In my office. Now."

Steeling himself for another round of threats, Damien followed Darius into the lushly appointed room, mildly surprised when the older man locked the door.

"Wouldn't want to be overheard," he said. Crossing to the window, he pulled the shades closed, then drew the curtains. "You should know I have this room periodically swept for electronic bugs or any kind of video-recording devices."

"A bit paranoid, aren't you?" Damien couldn't resist asking.

As expected, Darius frowned. "When you're a man in my position, you have to be."

"Really? And what position is that?"

"Enough already," Darius snarled. "I want to know what the FBI was doing here."

"Surely you're aware they're investigating you?"

Moving more swiftly than Damien had ever seen him move, Darius crossed the room until he stood toe-to-toe with his son.

"What did you tell them?"

Though he knew he was pushing it, Damien couldn't resist another jab. "What are you so worried about?"

Instead of answering, Darius cocked his graying head. "Let me say this. If you value that pretty little Kelley girl you've been nailing, you'll keep your mouth shut."

"That's it." Damien had had enough. "What the hell is wrong with you? Leave her out of this. Threatening me is one thing, but she's not involved in this at all."

Darius gave him a sly smile so cold it didn't even touch the flatness of his eyes. "You try to do anything to hurt me or betray this family, and the girl will die. Worse, I'll see to it that she suffers."

Stunned, Damien eyed the man who had sired him. No hint of humanity remained in his father's calculated gaze.

Damien realized Finn could run all the tests at his disposal and they wouldn't reveal any medical reason for their father's behavior. Darius was a sociopath and had no doubt always been one. He'd just never expressed it so violently before. He probably meant what he said and would have no compunction about torturing and killing an innocent woman.

Shaking his head, Damien turned and went to the door. Unlocking it, he turned and gave Darius a look he'd perfected in prison. "I take care of my own, understand?" Then without waiting for an answer, he left, closing the door behind him.

When he reached the safety of his own room, Damien unclenched his fists and realized he was shaking. He needed to talk to Wes and convince his brother that it was time for the sheriff's office to step in. His entire family appeared to be disintegrating around him. Damien, having lost fifteen long years that he could never get back, had come home halfway expecting things to be exactly the way they'd been when he'd gone to prison. Now, almost four months out and counting, he realized he'd been a fool.

His brothers had all found women they wanted to spend the rest of their lives with. People change, grow older and move on. Because of his time behind bars, he was the only one who hadn't.

In his room, he started to undress, then stopped. The walls of his room, an average-sized bedroom in the huge ranch house, felt as though they were closing in on him. Too close, too confining. He felt trapped, the way he had often felt while in prison.

Eve... No. He had to figure this out on his own.

If this were during the summer months, and claustrophobia was making his chest tighten, he'd simply saddle up one of the horses and go for a long ride. Now, he couldn't, because the forecast was for an arctic blast, with temperatures dipping well below freezing. The utter darkness compounded with the cold made riding after sundown impossible. Instead, he could walk to the barn and spend time with the horses, perhaps even ride in the covered arena. Or… Deciding, he snatched his car keys from the dresser. He'd go for a drive in his pickup and cruise the streets of his hometown with the stereo blaring. That had always made him feel better when he'd been a teenager. It shouldn't be any different at thirty-five.

But, although he found the hum of the truck's engine soothing, the feeling of nowhere to go unsettled him. After thirty minutes of aimless driving, passing by Eve's house twice, he found himself back at the Corner Bar. Since there were still a couple of hours until last call, the place was still open, even though the parking lot only had five or six cars.

A beer would taste mighty fine right about now.

Parking, he debated whether or not to go inside. Just as he was reaching for the handle to open the truck door, the bar's side door opened and his brother Wes came outside, accompanied by Agent Donatello and his henchman.

Chapter 11

What the hell. Keys clenched tightly in his fist, Damien froze. A knot settled in his stomach as he watched his brother the sheriff laughing with the man who, less than an hour before, had threatened him.

After a few more seconds of talking in the cold night air, Donatello and his partner got into their black sedan and drove away. Hands in pockets, breath making plumes of mist in the freezing air, Wes stood and watched them go, then made his way toward his own truck.

"Wes." Opening his door, Damien called him over. "What was that all about?"

Expression closed, Wes came over and climbed up into the truck next to Damien. "I was about to ask you the same thing. I still can't believe you were their inside informant."

Relief flooding him, Damien snorted. "They wish. They must have come to you right after they left the house."

"What happened?"

As succinctly as possible, Damien relayed the evening's events, including Darius's crazy threats and menacing behavior. "I'm beginning to think our father is a true sociopath."

"Whew." Sitting back in the seat, Wes rubbed the back of his neck. "If he is, that would mean he's dangerous, and I don't like to think that about my own father."

"Me neither. But something's going on with him. While he's been odd ever since I got home, things are getting worse fast. He's hiding something."

"I wonder what Darius knows that's got him so worried."

"You and me both."

A chime sounded and Wes checked his phone. "Lily," he said with a sheepish smile. "She's reminding me we have to be out at the ranch at the crack of dawn to help with the preparations for the big feast this weekend."

At Damien's inquisitive look, Wes laughed. "It's so good to have you home. Sometimes I forget you were gone so long. Tomorrow the preparations start for the annual Christmas lunch."

"Already?" At Wes's nod, Damien groaned. "Why so early?"

"Because it's huge now. You remember how every year on the Sunday before Christmas, no matter their faith or lack of—"

"The congregations of a bunch of churches get together for a holiday meal. I know, I remember."

"It's bigger now. Actually, the entire town of Honey Creek holds one huge celebratory service."

The tradition had started in the early eighties, when Mrs. Murphy and the ladies of the Lutheran Church had held a joint Christmas supper with the ladies of the Catholic and Baptist churches. Each had invited their respective congregations.

The next year, the small Pentecostal Church joined, as well as Honey Creek's lone nondenominational church. The annual event became so popular that by the end of the eighties, men and women of all faiths, including those who didn't even celebrate the holiday, attended.

"That's hard to believe. The last time I went, it was at the high-school cafeteria," Damien mused.

Wes laughed. "Not anymore. The dinner's grown so huge that for the last several years, the town uses the Colton ranch's indoor riding arena. That's what they're doing tomorrow, setting up rows of buffet tables and folding chairs and getting everything ready. We even had heating installed."

"But tomorrow's only Wednesday. That's a long way from Sunday."

"You've been gone fifteen years," Wes pointed out gently. "Like I said, the thing's blossomed and grown."

"Now I'm really looking forward to Sunday." Damien squeezed his brother's shoulder. "Thanks, man."

"Any time." Serious now, Wes checked his watch. "It's late. If I'm going to head out to the ranch at dawn tomorrow, I'd better go home and get some rest."

"Me, too." Suddenly weary, Damien told Wes goodbye and started the truck.

Driving home, he again turned down Eve's street and coasted to a stop in front of her house. Already he regretted storming out on her earlier. He needed to apologize, but her house was dark. Plus, he'd already shown up unannounced once tonight and didn't want to do so again.

Instead, he put the truck in Drive and headed home. He'd apologize to her tomorrow. He hoped she'd understand.

He rose the next morning a full hour before sunrise.

After showering and dressing, he padded down to the kitchen to make coffee and found Jeremy waiting, also fully dressed and munching on a stack of waffles.

"What are you doing up so early?" Damien asked, pouring a steaming cup of coffee.

"I can't wait." The teenager practically jumped up and down with excitement. "This year Uncle Duke said I could help park the cars. I might get to drive one and everything! It's going to be so wicked!"

Grinning back, Damien ruffled the boy's hair. "Let me drink a cup of coffee and grab a muffin. Then maybe we should head out to the barn and see if Sharon needs any help."

Barely concealing his impatience, Jeremy nodded. He fiddled in his chair while Damien ate, slurping at his glass of milk while Damien sucked down a second cup of coffee.

Finally, Damien stood. "Are you ready?"

The boy needed no second prompting. He ran for the coatrack, snatched off his parka and Damien's, then ran back to hand Damien his coat.

Chuckling, Damien bundled up against the winter morning.

Outside, even with the pole lights lit, the sky was still inky-black. Even at this early hour, a crew had already started getting the first field off the road ready to be turned into a massive parking lot. Metal gates, usually locked, stood wide open.

Wind buffeted them as they strode toward the barn. Though the air was cold and crisp, it was dry. The clear sky revealed several constellations sparkling like diamonds in the still-dark sky. With such a big event scheduled, Damien supposed it was a good thing they weren't expecting snow.

As they neared the barn, they saw what looked like close

to thirty people, mostly women, bustling around unloading boxes from two white panel vans. The barn opened to reveal people already hanging decorations inside.

No one noticed them, so engrossed were they in their own tasks.

Damien exchanged a look with Jeremy. "I don't think they need us," Damien said, surprised to see so many people already at work at such an early hour.

At that, Jeremy looked so disappointed that Damien relented. "Of course I'm sure there's always a spot for an extra hand."

But now Jeremy wasn't listening. He'd fixated all of his attention on a petite blonde girl in a hot-pink ski jacket and hat.

"Who's that?" Damien asked, hiding his amusement.

Jeremy tore his gaze away from the teenager to grin sheepishly at Damien. "Nobody. Just a girl from my school."

Cuffing the boy lightly on the shoulder, Damien let it go. "If you want to go help her, go ahead."

"Okay." Needing no second urging, Jeremy sauntered over to the shyly smiling girl.

Whistling under his breath, Damien went inside the barn. Christmas carols were playing from a portable stereo set up on a table. He wandered over to where three men were setting up a series of long buffet tables. They'd already done two rows of ten and were starting on a third.

"Need any help?"

The instant the men looked up, the easy camaraderie vanished from their faces. "No, thanks."

Studiously avoiding meeting his gaze, the trio went back to work.

Pretending it didn't bother him, Damien moved away. Even here, on his own ranch? Though it stung, this would be his first Christmas in fifteen years as a free man, and he refused to let anyone—especially small-minded fools—ruin it for him.

A second group of men were assembling small artificial Christmas trees. There had to be at least thirty boxes stacked near them. Approaching, Damien didn't ask this time. He just reached for a box and opened it, getting right to work, ignoring the way their carefree banter stopped, then started up again, haltingly, when he made no effort to join in.

"Hey, handsome!" A feminine voice called, barely discernable over the rowdy version of "Jingle Bell Rock" playing.

When he didn't turn, someone tugged on his sleeve.

Turning, his eyes locked with Eve's bright-blue ones, and his mouth went dry.

She didn't appear to notice. "When you get finished over here, will you come help me?"

Dumbstruck, he nodded. Had she already forgiven him for storming out the day before? "I'll help," he managed.

"Fantastic!" She smiled, sending his heart rate into double time. "I'm over there, unpacking napkins and paper plates, but I'm going to need someone to help me put the tablecloths on the tables once they're all set up."

"Give me a minute and I'll be there," he said, aware of the other men's interested stares. "I'm just about done with this tree."

With a nod and a wave, she moved off.

Finishing the tree in record time, he forced himself to stroll over slowly. When he reached Eve, she was rolling plastic cutlery sets inside holiday napkins.

"There you are." Reaching out, she touched his arm.

Hands in pockets, he nodded. "Listen, I need to apologize for what I said last night."

"No need." Her smile never wavered as she gestured around the room. "I saw how they treated you. I didn't understand before. Now I do. No worries."

He wanted to hug her. Not wanting to start gossip, he restrained himself.

In the course of the afternoon, as Eve dragged him from group to group, chore to chore, he realized she was single-handedly making sure everyone accepted his help and, more importantly, him.

She didn't know it, but she'd given him a present greater than gold.

Hours later, when all the tables were in place, and fifty artificial trees had been covered with white lights, everyone gradually left to go home. Damien stood next to Eve, watching his father's wife check on all the finishing details.

"Are you coming over later?" Eve asked him quietly. "I put fixings for beef stew in the slow cooker and made a loaf of bread in my bread machine."

Heart so full that it hurt, he nodded. "I'm starving." And he was, for more than food. "What time?"

"Give me an hour to shower."

He tried to hide his eagerness. "Do you want me to bring anything?"

For an answer, she winked. "Just your big ol', bad self."

Showering and changing in record time, Damien found himself in the truck on the way to Eve's house in forty-five minutes. He stopped at a small grocery store and purchased a bottle of alcohol-free wine. As he drove toward town he caught himself whistling, and he shook his head, grinning.

He parked in her driveway and his grin widened as Eve opened the front door before he'd made it halfway up the sidewalk. She'd changed from her jeans into a soft sweaterdress the same blue as her eyes. Her long blond hair was still damp from the shower. And her welcoming smile starting a slow burn of desire deep inside him.

"Hey," she said softly, stepping back to let him inside. He gave in to the impulse and kissed her.

When they broke apart, both were breathing heavily.

"Wow." Blinking up at him, she shook her head. "You're amazing."

"I was going to bring you a bottle of wine," he said. "But I remembered you couldn't drink it, so I brought this instead." He lifted the alcohol-free wine bottle, wishing he'd bought it earlier so he could have had Maisie put it into one of her fancy bags or something.

"Wonderful." Beaming at him, Eve carried the bottle into the kitchen. "This will be perfect with the beef stew."

"It smells great." Damien inhaled appreciatively. "Fresh baked bread and homemade stew. You can't ask for more than that."

At his compliments, Eve positively glowed. He followed her into the kitchen, where she had a perfectly set table with a large candle burning as a centerpiece.

"Do you need any help?" he asked.

"Nope. I've got it under control. Why don't you go sit in the den and I'll holler at you when it's ready to eat."

Though he didn't want to leave her side, he nodded and wandered into the other room. A fire blazed in the fireplace and he took a seat on an overstuffed chair, watching the flames and thinking.

This could be his life. Sharing this home with the woman.

If he hadn't been sent to prison, he'd probably be a dad by now, with a couple of kids and a life full of love.

An ordinary life. Something he hadn't even realized he craved until recently.

"It's ready," Eve called, breaking him out of his reverie.

As he took a seat at the table, it occurred to him that he'd been given a second chance. Being with Eve made the impossible possible.

The fragrant stew tasted delicious and the crusty French bread she'd made in her bread machine was the perfect complement. Damien had seconds, which clearly pleased her.

When they'd finished, he insisted on cleaning up and ordered her to take a seat by the fire. As soon as the last dish was stacked in the dishwasher, he joined her.

As he put his arm around her and side by side they leaned back, full and content, he felt a glimmer of hope brighter and stronger than anything he'd felt since being imprisoned.

Lost in his thoughts and enjoying the feeling of closeness, he looked down at Eve and realized she'd fallen asleep. Moving carefully, he covered her with a light blanket and let himself out of her house through the back door, since he could lock it behind him.

On the drive home he cursed his foolish optimism. It was all very well and good to hope for the future if you were an ordinary man. But with all his baggage, Damien knew that this would probably be only a dream for him. That didn't stop his chest from aching as he parked and went inside to go to bed alone, already missing Eve.

Finally the day of the big feast dawned. Montana weather, never the most reliable, gave them an early Christmas gift of clear skies and unseasonably warm temperatures, with a forecast of highs in the fifties.

All Honey Creek's shops and businesses closed early, and a great feeling of festivity filled the air. Outside, the men tended to the huge smokers, ensuring that the meat was cooked, while inside the arena the women set out tray after tray of cooked dressing, sweet-potato casserole, green beans and rolls.

As the celebration approached, most of the ranch hands were given a break from their daily chores. Working abbreviated three-hour shifts, they rode out in groups of three or four to check on the herd and the fence, and spent the rest of their time engaged in friendly poker games under Darius's radar.

Since the ranch hands had begun to treat him like one of their own, Damien tried to participate in the games. He wanted to relish the experience, so fresh and new after years of confinement, but although he'd honed his poker skills during the years in prison, he couldn't concentrate. He could think of nothing but Eve, her beautiful bright-blue eyes gazing so expectantly at him, her full lips curving in a smile. When they were last together, they couldn't stop touching each other.

He couldn't help but wonder if they'd sit together, which would mean she'd have to sit at the head table with the rest of his family. Her sister Susan would be there with Duke, as would his Wes's and Duke's fiancées. Of course, if Eve sat by his side, that would be akin to making a public statement, something they hadn't really discussed.

The other alternative, which he liked better, would be to sit with her among her family. Same statement, but less visible.

Or, he reflected glumly, they could sit separately, which would be the most sensible option if they didn't want gossip.

He didn't really care if people talked about him, but Eve was a different matter. He'd do what he had to do to protect her even if he didn't like it.

Eve arrived at the Colton Ranch an hour early, hoping to catch Damien alone, but as she waited in a long line of cars on the road leading to the ranch, she realized several others had chosen to come early as well.

Teenagers were hard at work directing cars to one of the two pastures designated for parking. After Eve pulled into her slot, she checked her reflection in the rearview mirror. Her new green sweater looked good with her blond hair and she'd tucked her jeans into a pair of furry boots.

One hand on the car door, she swallowed. Oddly enough, she felt nervous. Though she and Damien had been getting together nearly every single night, she wasn't sure how to act here at his home with the entire town watching.

Would they sit together? The entire Colton clan usually held court at a long, raised table in the front of the crowd. Her sister Susan would be up there this year, next to her fiancé, Duke Colton, as would Lily Masterson with Wes, and Rachel Grant with Finn, and the other Colton children, Joan, Brand and Perry. If Damien asked Eve to sit there, it would mark her as of special significance, something she wasn't sure she was ready or willing to accept.

No complications, she reminded herself. Damien understood that as well. All would be good. Still, that didn't stop her from wiping sweaty palms down the front of her jeans as she walked up to the barn.

Inside, townspeople milled around, gathering in small groups to talk. Some were claiming their seats, saving places for their friends and family. The only Colton she saw was Sharon, busy directing a small army in the placement of the large trays of food with their accompanying warmer candles.

Moving off into a corner, Eve pulled out her phone and sent him a text. *I'm here. Where are you?*

Look behind you, came back.

Slowly she turned. He stood in the entrance, alone, watching her. Her heart leapt into her throat and she had to forcibly restrain herself to keep from running into his arms.

Keeping her expression as casual as possible, she strolled over to him. "Hey, you."

"Hey, yourself." His velvet-brown gaze searched her face. "Want to sit together?"

Eve froze. "Up at your family's table?" she squeaked. "I don't…"

"We don't have to." He touched her arm, his fingers gentle. "If you don't want to sit up there, we can sit somewhere else."

For the first time she considered what this meant to him, that he was willing to give this up. For the first time in fifteen years, he had the right to sit with his siblings and his father at the family table. Eat with them, be with them, celebrate the holiday with those closest to him. And he wanted to give this up to be with her?

Part horrified, part humbled, she looked away. Her clan, with all her brothers and sisters and their spouses, as well as extended family, usually took up two entire tables. This time, her sister Susan would be eating up front with Wes. This was to be expected, since the two were engaged to be married.

But if Eve were to sit with Damien, people would assume…

When she dragged her gaze back to him, she saw an impassive cowboy, trying hard to pretend not to care. She knew this man and, as much as she might try to deny it, she cared about him. As a friend and...more. The realization both terrified and exhilarated her.

"I'll sit up front with you," she said, impulsively deciding. "It's time I stopped worrying so much about what people think."

Pure joy flashed across his face, so quickly she might have imagined it. He gave a slow nod, then took her hand, threading his large, calloused fingers through hers. Giving her a mischievous grin, he led her toward the front of the huge indoor arena.

"Let's really give them something to talk about," he said. Then he kissed her.

Time both stood still and rushed forward. For the space of several heartbeats she couldn't move, couldn't react, then the heat of his mouth moving across hers seared her, bringing her to life.

"Ahem." Someone cleared a throat behind them, yanking Eve right back to her surroundings. Face flaming, she pushed away and looked up, straight into her mother's curious face.

"Bonnie Gene." Damien stepped forward. "Sorry about that. Eve looks so pretty, I just had to kiss her."

If the ground could have opened up and swallowed her, Eve would have taken a nose dive for it. "Hi, Mom."

Ignoring Eve, her mother looked Damien up and down. "Staking a claim?" she asked, eyes twinkling.

He gave her a wicked grin. "Maybe I am."

She nodded. "Good." Without another word, she turned and walked away.

Shocked, Eve stared after her. "What the heck was that about?"

His grin widened, inviting her to join in. "I think your mother just gave me her stamp of approval."

Shaking her head, Eve began to move forward, not touching him this time. "Let's go find our seats."

"Regretting your decision?" he asked, his voice suddenly serious. "Because if you are…"

"You'll let me go back and sit with my mother? How fun would that be now?"

"No. I was going to say that I'm not letting you out of it." He took her arm, ignoring her resistance. "Sweetheart, if you're going to do something, you might as well do it up right."

With that, he led her up to the front. As she took her seat next to him at the long table, she felt a bit like royalty of olden times. Banishing the feeling, she smiled at Finn and Rachel, just arriving.

Damien got up to talk to Finn, and Eve took the time alone to calm herself. She'd never been a coward and hated that she felt so nervous now. It wasn't as though she and Damien actually were an item.

The room began to fill up as more and more townspeople arrived. Sharon Colton, still busy making sure the serving lines were set up correctly, would be one of the very last to take her seat. Her husband, Darius, would, as usual, make a grand entrance and once he made it to the front, he'd tap on his wineglass to get everyone's attention. Only when the room became completely and utterly silent, would he announce it was time to eat.

After that, pandemonium would reign.

"What are you doing here?" Her sister, Susan, appeared behind Eve, eyes wide. "I saw you sitting up here all by yourself and thought I'd better rescue you. Mom and the rest of the clan are at our usual table," she hinted.

Fidgeting, Eve felt like a little kid. "I'm here with Damien." There. She'd said it.

Smile faltering, Susan did a double take. "With Damien? Colton? Are you sure?"

Just then Damien came up behind them. Putting his hand possessively on Eve's shoulder, he smiled. "Hi, Susan. Where's Duke?"

"He, uh, went to see if Jeremy needed any help parking the cars." She darted a look from Damien to Eve and back again. "Eve says you're here together?" Voice rising on the last word, she made this sound like they'd just announced they were submitting to bizarre experimental drug testing in the Yucatan.

Glancing from one sister to the other, Damien frowned. Only the quirk at one corner of his mouth told Eve he was trying not to crack up. "Yes, we're together. Why? Do you have a problem with that?"

Susan immediately began backtracking. "Er, no. It's just that I didn't know Eve was seeing anyone. And I don't think Duke even knows you're dating Eve." She began looking around wildly, trying to find her fiancé. "We need to bring him over here and fill him in, don't you think?"

Trying to keep from laughing was a battle and Eve finally lost it. "Susan," she managed between chortles, "relax. Damien and I are just good friends."

Before anyone could say another word, the rest of the Coltons hurried to their places. A commotion at the entrance to the arena let everyone know that Darius was preparing to make his grand entrance.

And, exactly as he'd done every other year, he did. Moving up the center aisle, shaking hands on one side and then the other, and basking in the adulation as if he were a rock star. Completely used to this, Eve sat back and watched, amused. Beside her, she felt Damien's sudden tension and remembered he'd been in prison for the last fifteen years. The entire production, with its familiar ceremony and almost ritualistic feel, would seem strange to him.

She wondered what he'd done while in prison. Thinking this made her realize how little he talked about his experiences there. Maybe because the memories were too painful.

Then Darius climbed the steps to the platform and the Colton family table. As he made his way to his seat in the center, his gaze locked on Eve, and the hard look in his eyes wasn't the least bit friendly. In fact, he looked downright dangerous.

Chapter 12

Luckily, Sharon Colton bustled up to the table next, drawing Darius's gaze away from Eve. Troubled, Eve looked down at her plate, wondering if she'd imagined the disturbing malice in the look the Colton patriarch had given her. Surely she must have. After all, what reason would the head of the Colton family have to dislike her? If it was because she was a Kelley, she'd think her sister Susan would draw more of his ire—especially since Susan was actually marrying his son Duke. Eve was merely Damien's guest.

Darius intoned the traditional blessing, finishing as he always did, with a request to form lines at the buffet. When he turned to take his seat, his gaze drifted impersonally over his collective family, before narrowing on Eve.

Again, she felt the force of his glare. Telling herself it was due to an overactive imagination didn't help—not when the man kept shooting her venom-filled looks. Resolving to ask Damien later, Eve decided to let it go for now.

Next to her, Damien talked with his twin brother, Duke, her own sister's fiancé. Eve forced herself to relax, leaning back in her chair and watching as the crowd surged to form lines near the self-serve buffet tables. A veritable army of servers stood by, carving meat and constantly refilling trays of food, making sure everything was hot.

The Coltons, as hosts of the banquet, had the right to go to the head of either line whenever they wanted. Maisie and Jeremy went first, followed by Finn and Rachel and Wes and Lily. Duke and Susan, contentedly holding hands, waited a few minutes longer until the first group came back with their plates.

"Are you coming?" Duke asked Damien, giving Eve a friendly smile.

"In a minute," Damien answered, his voice tense. With a nod, Duke moved off, one arm around Susan.

"What's wrong?" Eve murmured, wondering if Damien, too, had noticed his father's odd behavior.

"Nothing." He smiled, but it didn't reach his eyes. "Are you ready?" Though he asked the question in a light voice, Damien touched her arm, as if giving her a warning.

Dubious, she glanced around him to where Darius and Sharon still stood, like benevolent rulers surveying their kingdom. As ashamed as she would be to admit it out loud, she was afraid if she moved that she'd once again draw Darius's cold stare.

"I'm not sure," she admitted with a slight grimace. "Shouldn't your father and stepmother go first?"

Glancing at him, she saw him eyeing his father, who now had started once again to glower in their direction.

"What's the matter with him?" she asked. "Is he mad about me being here?"

"Who knows?" His attempt to sound unconcerned fell flat, especially since he tightened his arm around her. "He's been acting kind of weird lately. It's probably best if we ignore it. Do you want to eat?"

She nodded, getting slowly to her feet at the same time as Damien. Trying to avoid glancing out into the crowd, she still felt as if she had a hundred pairs of eyes on her, many of them mirroring the disapproval she'd seen in Darius's. No doubt the gossip had already started.

She told herself she didn't care, reminding herself she'd better get used to being an object of scandal. The speculation and rumors would start to swirl in earnest once people realized she was pregnant. And when she refused to reveal the father or the circumstances concerning her pregnancy, the rumors would become outrageous. At some point she expected to be asked if her baby had been fathered by aliens. No lie.

As Damien turned to help lead the way down, a shadow fell over the table. After pushing her chair back in, Eve looked up. Darius had stepped in front of them, back to the crowd, completely blocking their way down.

"Son, aren't you going to introduce your little friend?" Darius asked, tone dripping venom.

Wary, Eve instinctively moved closer to Damien as he performed a quick introduction.

"Pleased to meet you," Darius said, sounding anything but. Giving her hand a quick squeeze, the older man quickly released it, returning his attention to his son.

"Well, well, well. I wasn't aware you were this serious," Darius smirked. "Good for me, bad for you."

Though his words made no sense, Damien's sudden tense grip on her arm told Eve that he at least understood what his father meant by the odd statement.

"Don't even go there," Damien warned. "This isn't about her."

"You keep your nose out of my business, and I'll keep

mine out of yours." Suddenly affable, Darius held out his hand. "Deal?"

Stone-faced, Damien made no move to accept his father's offer.

As the silence stretched out, Darius's smile faded. Finally, he lowered his arm, his expression going hard again. "I should have known. So that's the way it's going to be?"

"Excuse us," Damien said firmly, steering Eve around his father. "We're going to go eat."

Darius stepped aside without a word.

On the way down, they passed the others returning. Even though Damien stood protectively close, Eve swore she could still feel Darius's rancor-filled gaze burning into her back.

"What was that all about?" she asked softly as they made their way toward the buffet table.

"I'll tell you later." Squeezing her arm in a too-hard gesture that he'd no doubt meant to be reassuring, he gave her a smile tinged with anger.

Filling her plate with the piping-hot food, Eve tried and failed to recapture her earlier contentment. The look in Damien's father's eyes had been tinged with madness, a very real, almost feral look that seemed as dangerous as an actual physical threat.

No one else appeared to have noticed a thing. Following Damien's lead, she smiled and chatted with several people in the serving line, ignoring the question in many of their gazes. None of them were quite bold enough to ask her outright why she was sitting with the Coltons, but she knew that would wear off by Tuesday. In fact, she anticipated twice the amount of traffic in her hair salon, with women stopping by just to "visit."

Plates filled, she and Damien made their way back to

their seats. Throughout the entire meal, despite the friendly overtures made by Damien's brothers, she couldn't help but feel conscious of Darius's hostile glare, especially since he sent it her way every time she looked toward him.

When they'd finished eating, pastors of the various churches announced the date, time and meeting location for each of their annual Christmas carol sings. The Coltons' church traditionally had theirs Christmas Eve, with caroling that afternoon, before the holiday service.

Sitting at the front table was a completely different experience for Eve. Her family's table, situated in the thick of things, usually ended up empty as various family members socialized with their friends and neighbors. Once everyone had eaten, they roamed, standing in small clusters and talking, before moving on to the next group.

The Coltons were different. As if they were forbidden to leave, not a single one of them left their seats. Instead, everyone came to them, swarming the table like bees to a hive. Bemused, Eve caught her sister's eye. Susan shrugged and went back to looking for her friends so she could wave them over.

Meanwhile, the food was cleared and trays of desserts brought in. Pumpkin, pecan and apple pies, and there had to be at least ten cakes, most baked by the attendees. When all had been set out, along with coffee, many people went for the sweets while others continued to visit.

All in all, Eve thought, a pleasant way to spend an afternoon. In the past, this particular event had been the galvanizing event to give her a dose of the holiday spirit.

This year should have been no different, but as she glanced uneasily at Darius, holding court over his cronies, she realized it had been. If it weren't for Damien, she would have scurried back to her own family like a chastened mouse. Instead, she sat calmly, viewing a group of six dowagers from her mother's quilting club who were bearing down on her. The glint in their eyes promised she was in for the kind of grilling only a true gossip hound can produce.

As if he saw them coming, Damien put his arm around her and joined her in facing them. This didn't slow them one bit in their determined progress and Eve steeled herself for the questions.

To her surprise, just as they approached the table, Sharon Colton stepped in front of them, asking them something about the Christmas-caroling committee.

"Divertive missile launched," Damien muttered dryly. "You are so lucky."

Watching as Sharon led them away, Eve couldn't help but laugh. "Yes, I am."

As the afternoon wore on, more and more people took their leave. Bonnie Gene came up and gave both Eve and Susan a hug before leaving.

"You look good together," she whispered in Eve's ear, indicating Damien with a thumbs-up sign.

To her dismay, Eve felt her face flush. "Thanks," she managed.

A few minutes after her family left, finally Eve felt as if it was time to go.

"Are you ready?" Damien asked, making her wonder if he'd read her mind.

She nodded, keeping her head high as she rose, feeling Darius's malevolent glare on her back all the way to the door.

Damien followed her home in his truck.

Max greeted him in the enthusiastic way boxers have, overjoyed to see his new friend. Eve measured out her dog's kibble, then, while he ate, she poured two glasses of nonalcoholic wine and carried them into her living room, where Damien had lit a fire.

"This is nice." Accepting the glass, Damien sat on the couch, stretching his legs. "You were a trouper today."

"Thanks. I actually enjoyed it," she said honestly. "Except for the weirdness with your father. What was all that about?"

What he told her next stunned her.

"Your own father stole your inheritance?"

"Not just mine, but possibly my brothers' and sisters', too." He looked grim, taking a long drink of wine. "And when I asked him about it, he threatened me."

"What do you mean? Threatened you how?"

"Like he wanted to kill me." The bleakness in his deep voice tugged at her memory.

"You know, Sharon said something similar when she was in for her hair appointment the other day. She said she was worried her own husband was trying to kill her."

"Since he attacked her with a fireplace poker, I'm not surprised. Something's got to be done about Darius, but I don't know what. We've had a family meeting about it, but nothing got resolved."

Though hesitant to do so, she knew she should tell him everything she knew. "You know, I've heard the FBI is investigating him. No one in town is sure what for, but that's the ongoing rumor." She lifted one shoulder in a shrug, just to show he shouldn't take her seriously.

To her surprise, he did. "They *are* investigating him. Racketeering and money-laundering are just two of the items they've mentioned. They actually approached me about being an informant."

Her mouth fell open. "On your own father?"

"Yes," he said bitterly. "On my own father. What's worse, at one point I actually considered it.

Hurriedly, she took a sip of her drink, trying to compose her expression. "You did?"

"At one point. But not now. Darius's problems are family business. If he's broken the law, they'll need to prove it without my help."

Aching, she touched his arm. "You sound as though you think he has."

"Broken the law?" He gave a harsh laugh. "A man who would steal from his own son? I have no doubt Darius has done things he should go to prison for. But I've been in prison, and no matter how evil he seems to be, I wouldn't wish that on any man, especially not my own father."

"It must have been awful for you," she said softly. Sitting shoulder to shoulder, hip to hip.

Staring off into the distance, he didn't respond. The pain etched in his rugged face tore at her heart.

She loved this man. The realization hit her like a lightning bolt, so awful and glorious and strong she had to push herself up off the couch. When had this happened and how? Galvanized into motion, she strode into the kitchen, needing the comforting ritual of making coffee, something, anything, to keep her hands busy and purge her mind.

"I should go," he said from behind her.

For one terrible instant she froze, on the verge of unreasonable and unwarranted tears. Then, getting a grip on herself, she nodded, making herself turn and face him with a completely insincere smile.

"I am kind of tired," she lied. Throat aching, she managed to keep the smile in place as he uncoiled himself from the sofa and headed toward her.

"One kiss." Low-voiced, more of a command than a request.

She could do this. She could, without giving herself away. Walking into his arms was easy, as was lifting her face to his. But when his mouth covered hers, soft and warm, familiar and beloved, her self-restraint vanished.

Now fully aware of her feelings, heat and passion flooded her. Her burning desire ignited his own, and they wound up back on the couch, naked limbs intertwined, making love with such a deep yet tender urgency that she wanted to weep.

When it was over he held her, silent. Lying in his arms felt good and right, making her hate herself for betraying her own rules. No strings. They'd both agreed. Worse, she knew if she told him her feelings had changed, he'd run fast and far. So she kept her mouth shut, cherishing the feel of him, and steeled herself for the moment when he had to leave.

As if he sensed her turbulent emotions, he kissed her softly before easing out of her arms. "Don't worry so much."

Startled, she stared at him. "What do you mean?"

"I can see it in your face. You're worried about something. If it's my father, don't be. He has as little as possible to do with my life, and vice versa."

Relieved, and feeling somewhat better, she nodded. "Okay." She swallowed, then gathering up her nerve, she said, "Stay."

"Not tonight," he said, kissing her hard on the lips. "But I'll take a rain check, okay?"

She nodded, wishing she didn't feel so foolish.

Dressing hurriedly, he left, giving her one final kiss before breezing out the door.

Smiling to herself, she watched until his taillights disappeared. Then, locking the front door, she turned and made her way back to her bedroom, intent on trading her clothes for a comfortable pair of well-worn sweats. At the last minute, she remembered she needed to let Max in, so she detoured to the back door.

Shaking off snow, the big dog bounded in. Laughing at her pet's antics, Eve finally gave him a bully stick to settle him down. The fire had burned down to embers and she banked these, yawning.

Damien had barely left and already she missed him. She could get used to having him around. Pulling herself up, she gave herself a sharp talking-to. She didn't love him—she couldn't love him. Having relationship hopes always led to disappointment and pain. She'd sworn she wouldn't do this again, not with him. Especially not with him.

Distracted, she prowled around her house, putting everything back in its place, rinsing out the wineglasses before placing them in the dishwasher.

Satisfied that her tidy little world was back in order—this was one of the few things she *could* control—she whistled for the dog and padded off to bed.

Max circled three times before settling into his dog bed. She pulled back the covers and got her own bed ready, before brushing her teeth and washing her face.

Abstractedly—for curiosity's sake only—she allowed herself to wonder what it would be like to climb into her bed at the end of a day with a warm and drowsy Damien waiting for her. Cutting off the thought because the rush of pleasure it brought alarmed and worried her, she climbed beneath the covers and turned off the light.

Sometime later, Max's low growling from his bed woke her. Instantly alert, she lay still in her bed and listened.

Max sprang to his feet, entire body tense. He took a step forward, lips lifted in a snarl.

"Wait," she ordered softly. Sliding her feet into her slippers, she grabbed her robe from the end of the bed and moved slowly toward the doorway. Honey Creek had been virtually crime-free her entire life. No robberies, break-ins or assaults. Certainly, other than the Mark Walsh case, no murders. Of course, there had been cases of various kinds of wildlife crashing into people's homes—deer, moose, bird, even the occasional mountain lion or bear.

She suspected this might be just such an instance.

Though she'd trained Max well and didn't think he'd disobey her commands, she closed the bedroom door, shutting him in. If the intruder was larger than her dog, she didn't want to take a chance that Max would be injured or killed.

Moving carefully, as any wild animal was sure to already be in panic mode, when she came to the curve in the staircase, she peered around the side to below. Eyes already adjusted to the darkness, she froze at the sight below.

A tall shadow, human rather than animal, stood silhouetted below. Male, stocky, wearing a black hoody. And holding something that looked like a crowbar or a baseball bat.

As she registered these details, the man lifted his weapon and swung, shattering her flat-screen TV. Heart pounding, she tried to catch her breath, cursing the fact that she hadn't grabbed a cordless phone or her cell. Moving back into the shadows, she watched as he took out her lamps next, then the Christmas tree, walloping the branches until he'd shattered just about every single ornament. Branches cracked and snapped and her beautiful tree looked whipped and beaten.

At some point it dawned on her that he wasn't taking any pains to be quiet or hide the fact that he was systematically destroying her home. Which meant he didn't care if she caught him, in fact he'd probably welcome the chance to hurt or even kill her.

Why? Cradling her stomach protectively, Eve backtracked her steps, moving swiftly. Once in the relative safety of her bedroom, she locked her door and released Max from his stay, uncomfortably aware that her seventy-five-pound dog might be her—and her unborn child's—only protection.

Snarling louder, as if he sensed her distress, Max faced the doorway. With the hair on his back raised, he looked ready to attack. Keeping her eye on the door, Eve snatched up the phone and heard the dial tone with relief; part of her had assumed the intruder would have taken out the phone line. She punched the number for the sheriff's office.

A second later, Wes Colton's dispatcher came on the line. Speaking in a hushed voice, Eve urgently relayed the situation and begged them to hurry.

Once she'd hung up, still clutching the phone, she searched her bedroom for something to use as a weapon, pitifully aware of her shortcomings in the self-defense department. The best she could come up with was a large, heavy flashlight.

Through the closed bedroom door, she could still hear crashes, telling her the man was still savagely wrecking her belongings. Though the thought stung, better that he struck inanimate objects rather than her or Max. Still, why? What had she done to make someone that angry? This didn't make sense.

Suddenly conscious of the phone still gripped in her hand, Eve dialed Damien's cell. He answered on the second ring.

"Miss me already?" he teased.

Tersely, she told him what was going on. "I called 911 so Wes or one of his guys should be here soon."

"I'm on my way. I'll be there in ten," he told her. "Stay

put. Don't leave your bedroom, okay?" He hung up without waiting for an answer.

Knowing rescue was on the way didn't settle her nerves. She could still see the man in his black hoody swinging his crowbar, as if the image had been permanently burned on her eyeballs.

Why, why, why? She rubbed her eyes.

A few seconds went by without any crashing sounds. Then a few more. Outside, a motor roared to life. Motorcycle? Hurrying to the window, Eve saw the taillights of some kind of big bike flash red before disappearing into the distance.

After that, everything seemed to happen at once. The sound of sirens growing closer, flashing lights—red and blue—as two Honey Creek squad cars pulled into her drive.

Voices yelling, a crash, a shout, Max barking wildly, all the while she stood in her darkened bedroom, unable to move except to tremble.

Downstairs, the police called her name, alternating between *Eve* and *Miss Kelley*. Still she could do nothing but clutch her flashlight so hard her hands hurt and stare at the door.

Max went into protective dog overdrive, launching himself at the door, snarling and growling. Still she stood frozen, a statue of shock. Only when she heard Damien's voice calling her name could she take a deep breath and move forward, moving Max back and putting him on the down command, then stay. Though the tension in the boxer's body showed he really didn't want to obey, he'd been well-trained and so he did.

Opening her door slowly, she peered out. Downstairs she could hear men's voices, recognizing Wes and one of his deputies, Charlie Calhoun. And Damien, calling her as he ran for the stairs, taking them two at a time. As he rounded the curve, barreling up to the landing, she launched herself into his arms.

"Are you all right?" He smoothed back her hair, kissing her cheek and her neck and finally her mouth. "Jesus, Eve. Downstairs looks like a tornado went through it. Did he touch you?"

"No, no." She hastened to reassure him, unable to stop her trembling even now. "I'm so glad you came."

"There's something you need to see."

Tempted to refuse, to hide her face and try to withdraw like a turtle seeking a shell, she nodded. Sooner or later she'd have to deal with what had happened, and she sure as heck would rather face this with Damien by her side.

With Damien holding her arm, she slowly descended the stairs. Stopping at the bottom to look up at him.

"This way," he told her, steering her toward the living room.

Tell him to leave town, or else.

Staring at the six-inch black letters written in marker on her living-room wall, Eve flinched. Only Damien's solid body behind her kept her steady on her feet.

"Any idea what that means?" Wes Colton asked, his voice gentle.

Speechless, Eve shook her head.

"What about you, Damien?" Wes pushed.

"No idea," Damien answered, deadpan. Glancing up at him, Eve knew instantly he was lying. He knew exactly what this meant.

Following this thought, an image of Darius Colton and his malicious glare popped into her head. Had Damien's father had something to do with the break-in? The idea seemed so ludicrous she nearly dismissed it, but a niggling seed of doubt told her she'd better discuss it with Damien later, when his brother the sheriff wasn't around.

"Take a look around, Eve," Wes said gently. "See if anything is missing."

Nothing was. Her belongings had been shredded and destroyed.

"Seems like it was personal," Wes commented, watching her closely.

"Maybe, but I can't imagine who would do such a thing. I have no enemies."

"That you know of."

Looking around at the mess that had been her living room, Eve had to agree. "That I know of."

Once the report had been written up and the scene processed, Wes and his deputy helped Damien tape up the back window while Eve vacuumed up pieces of glass. After one more circuit around the house looking for clues, Wes and his deputy climbed into their cars and left.

As soon as the police were gone, Damien pulled out his cell phone.

"What are you doing?" Eve asked, blinking.

"Calling that sorry SOB." Expression furious, he punched in a number. Listening, he shook his head and disconnected the call. "It went straight to voice mail. I'll talk to him personally when I get home."

She sighed, feeling stunned and strangely detached. Must be shock setting in. "You don't know for sure it was him."

A muscle worked in his jaw. "Oh, yeah? Who else would have done this? He wants me out of here. But he should know that I can't leave without my money."

"But to give you a warning through me? How is that effective?"

Pulling her into his arms, he kissed the top of her head. "Because it's a barely veiled double threat, sweetheart. He's letting me know he's not above hurting the people I care about to get me to leave."

"I don't understand."

"My inheritance is missing and Darius is worried that the Feds are investigating him. He's even threatened to have me killed."

Shocked, she gasped. "Your own father?"

"I think he's losing his grip on reality," he said. "Though I hate making excuses for him, that's the only explanation that makes sense."

"I can't stay here now," she told him. "Will you wait while I grab a few things? I'm going to spend the night with my mother."

"That's an excellent idea." He hugged her again. "Though I don't think you're in any real danger now that the message has been given. I want you to be safe. Do you want me to drive you?"

"No." She shook her head and pushed out of his arms. "I need to have my own vehicle. I'll be fine."

Still, he followed her all the way over to Bonnie Gene's, driving off only once she'd stepped inside. Eve couldn't help but wonder what would happen once he got to the ranch. She had no doubt he meant to confront his father. Closing her eyes, she prayed he'd be safe.

Chapter 13

On the drive back to the ranch, Damien struggled to get a grip on his rage. He believed he'd successfully hidden his fury from Eve. Somehow he'd kept his voice calm even when he'd wanted to explode.

Someone hurting Eve was a thousand times worse than anything Damien had ever imagined. He knew without a shred of doubt that Darius had been behind the break-in and the message. Threatening Eve. Pregnant, vulnerable, beautiful Eve.

How. Dare. He.

Pulling up fast, tires crunching on gravel, he parked under the barn light, strode to the house and threw open the front door.

"I know what you're thinking." Materializing from the shadows, Wes stepped into his path. "But Darius isn't here. I've already checked."

This stopped Damien in his tracks. "Where the hell is he?"

"Billings. He left right after the luncheon to go Christmas shopping."

Damien swore. "How freakin' convenient for him."

"Yeah." Hunched against the cold, Wes accompanied his brother into the house.

"His cell phone goes directly to voice mail."

"I know. I tried to call him, too. Sharon said he's probably visiting his mistress."

Damien shook his head as the two men headed inside. "Now, why doesn't that surprise me?"

"What, that he has a mistress or that Sharon knows about her?"

"Both. Damn. Nothing about him should shock me. Anyone who'd threaten a pregnant woman—" Too late he realized his mistake.

"Eve's pregnant?" Wes cocked his head. "Yours?"

"I shouldn't have said that. As a matter of fact, forget I did."

"You didn't answer the question."

Swearing, Damien turned away. When he faced his brother again, he took a deep breath before speaking. "That wasn't my secret to tell. So no, I won't be answering the question. Can we get back to Darius and what the son of a bitch did?"

"You don't know that it was him."

"Like hell I don't. You know as well as I do that he hired someone to do his dirty work for him. He conveniently left town to give himself an alibi."

"Again, you have no proof." Wes crossed his arms. "None of us needs to be jumping to hasty conclusions that have no basis in fact."

"Oh, come on." Damien rounded on his brother. "You know as well as I do that the old man's behind this."

"No, I don't. Yes, I agree it seems probable—"

"Probable? Who else would have done such a thing?"

Ignoring him, Wes continued. "We can take hunches, guesses and probabilities under consideration. But that's all we can do. Until we have proof—cold hard facts—we can't go off half cocked." Wes gave him a hard look. "Understand?"

Without agreeing, Damien relayed what had happened earlier at the Christmas luncheon.

"He *threatened* you?" Wes sounded as if he didn't believe it.

"And Eve. What about your need for proof now?"

"It makes a difference. I will have to talk to him about this."

"When?"

Wes shrugged. "When he gets back."

"But—"

Rounding on him, Wes looked as if he wanted to take a swing at Damien's jaw. As furious as he felt now, Damien thought he'd probably welcome it.

"I'm not going up to Billings to hunt him down." Wes swore. "Do you have any idea how it's going to feel, questioning my own father?"

"Do you have any idea how it feels being threatened by my own father?" Damien shot back.

They each took a deep breath, striving for calm. When Wes spoke again, he sounded curt and professional.

"Actually, no, I don't. Darius has never threatened me or, to my knowledge, anyone else in our family before this. But I do know we can only operate on facts, not on guesswork."

Damien managed a small smile. "That's the law-enforcement officer in you."

"Yes, but that's also the realist in me. Come on, Damien. This is your *father*. You got sent to prison based on circumstantial evidence. You of all people should know how it feels to be wrongfully convicted."

This brought Damien up short. He started to argue, changed his mind then shook his head. "What can I say? Darius has all but admitted he's behind this."

"Has he? Has our father admitted to breaking and entering and terrorizing your girlfriend?"

"No, but—"

Relentlessly, Wes cut him off. "Has Darius admitted to stealing your inheritance or laundering money?"

"Not in so many words."

"Then you have nothing. Without proof, it's all just as circumstantial as the evidence they used to convict you of a crime you didn't commit."

With that parting shot, Wes grabbed his coat, lifted his hand in farewell and left, leaving Damien sitting alone in front of the Christmas tree.

The next morning Maisie confronted Damien in the kitchen, catching him as he was pouring his first cup of coffee. Today she was wearing a soft brown sweaterdress and over-the-knee, high-heeled boots. Without her makeup, she looked like a cross between a Victoria's Secret model and the big sister he remembered from their childhood.

"What's going on with you and Eve Kelley?" she demanded.

He rolled his eyes. "Nosy, aren't you? How's Gary Jackson?"

"Touché."

He grinned, watching as she poured herself a cup of coffee, liberally spooning sugar and cream into it before stirring and taking a sip.

"However," she said, slowly raising her gaze to meet his, "I didn't invite Gary to sit at our table at the Christmas luncheon. You know what that means. The entire town will be talking."

Confused, he frowned. "She sat with me because we're together. We like each other. Nothing more than that."

"Have you bought her a ring?"

"What?" Damien let his mouth fall open. "Of course not."

"Well, you've just proved to the entire town that you're serious about her. No Colton invites a woman to sit at the family table for the Christmas luncheon unless they're engaged or married. You know that."

Did he? "Maybe that rule came into place while I was locked up," he finally said. "Why didn't she tell me?"

Maisie looked at him for a long second. "I don't know. Maybe she's hoping for a ring."

The thought sucked the breath from his chest and made him dizzy. He took a drink from his coffee mug to steady himself. Remembering Eve's attempt to tell him why she didn't want to sit with him, and his own reaction, he knew that wasn't the case.

Before he could summon up something to say, Maisie dropped another bombshell. "Damien, I need your help with something. You know I had an affair with Mark Walsh fifteen years ago? Should I tell Jeremy that he's Mark's son?"

Damien could only stare. Sometimes he felt as though he'd been dropped into a carnival fun house filled with twists and turns. "You and Mark Walsh?"

"Yes. It went on for over a year, right before he was supposedly murdered. I thought he loved me. He said I was irresistible but he was scared of my craziness, as he called it. Turns out he also had another lover in Costa Rica."

A horrible thought occurred to Damien. "Did you know

he wasn't really dead?" The depths of such a betrayal would destroy him.

"Of course not." Maisie looked at him as if he'd suddenly grown horns and a tail. "Do you honestly think I could have known that and let you rot in prison for fifteen years?"

Relief flooding him, Damien managed a shaky smile. "No. Sorry. I had to ask." Then another thought occurred to him. "That son of a bitch knew you were expecting his child and he still faked his own death?"

"No. I didn't find out I was pregnant until after his supposed murder.

"What about Darius? I'm guessing he was not too supportive."

"He was furious. It would have been ten times worse if he'd known who the father was. He wanted me to give up the baby. That's the only time in my life I've ever really stood up to him."

"You never told him Mark Walsh was Jeremy's father?"

"Nope. And Jeremy doesn't know either."

"Surely he's asked by now."

"Oh, yes." She gave him a wistful smile. "Many times. I keep telling him I don't want to talk about it."

"But now you want to tell him? Why?"

When she met his gaze, hers was direct and clear and honest. "Because I think he has the right to know. He's fourteen, old enough to handle it."

"But there's more, isn't there?"

"Maybe." She gave him a wistful smile. "I've been told that secrets are like poison to people like me."

"True enough." Damien didn't know if he should congratulate her on her insight or ask for specifics on who was advising her.

"That's why I've been trying to get that TV show, *Dr.*

Sophie, to get a camera crew out to Honey Creek. They need to reveal all the secrets."

"Are you still obsessed with that?" he asked.

"No. I've finally realized that they're only going to continue to ignore me. Apparently TV-watching America isn't interested in the goings-on of a small town in Montana."

"You're probably right," he agreed. "I've got to tell you, sis, I'm really glad you gave that one up."

"Whatever." She shrugged. "So I'm asking your opinion," Maisie continued. "What would be the best way to tell Jeremy the truth about his father?"

"Wait until he asks. Don't rush it, make him sit down and tell him slowly, but talk to him like he's a man."

"He is. My little man." She laughed. "Will you tell him for me?"

Only Maisie could ask such a thing and be serious.

"No." Reaching out, Damien touched her shoulder. "That's between the two of you. I can't be involved."

"I thought you'd say that." She sipped her coffee. "But it was worth a shot."

Time to change the subject.

"Wes said Darius is gone. When did he leave?" he asked as casually as he could manage.

"Right after the Christmas luncheon. He said he was going to do all of his Christmas shopping in Billings. Why?"

"Somebody broke into Eve's place last night while she was asleep in bed. They trashed it pretty good and left a message on her wall."

Maisie's jaw dropped. "Are you serious?"

"Deadly serious."

She closed her mouth. "What kind of message?"

He told her.

"And you think Darius is behind it."

Instead of answering right away, he refilled his coffee mug. "Yeah, I do. Don't you?"

She shrugged. "I don't know. It all seems kind of pointless. I mean, you and Eve aren't serious or anything, so why threaten her?" Narrowing her eyes, she studied him. "Unless Darius knows something I don't."

"Darius knows nothing about me or my life." He thought of something else Eve had said. "Wes said he talked to Sharon last night, and she said something about Darius being with his mistress. Do you know anything about that?"

Making an inelegant snorting noise, Maisie made a face at him. "Looking for something to use against him? Don't waste your time. Everyone knows about Darius's little 'indiscretions,' as he calls them. He *always* has a mistress, though none of them lasts long. He'll have a new one by February."

"Have you seen Sharon lately?"

"No, why?"

He relayed what Eve had told him Sharon had mentioned while having her hair done.

"Damien," Maisie said with exaggerated patience. "You saw him attack her with a fireplace poker. Of course she'd say he's trying to kill her."

"But that was an isolated incident, wasn't it? He was drunk. So was she."

"Like that excuses it?" Maisie huffed. "And for your information, that was not an isolated incident."

Damien stared. "You've seen others?"

"Not that violent, but yes. I've witnessed a thousand small cruelties. So has Jeremy. And remember the cigarette thing, how Darius made my son eat an entire pack of cigarettes."

"So Darius is off his rocker," Damien said glumly. "Finn's supposed to get him to allow tests. Until then, that doesn't mean we have to excuse his behavior."

"No, of course not." A tinge of bitterness colored Maisie's tone. "No one excuses mine."

Gently, he put his arm around her slender shoulders. "Maise, I know you don't think you need it, but have you thought about getting help?"

This time, instead of automatically shaking her head or getting angry, Maisie nodded. "I talked to Finn. He doesn't think I'm bipolar."

Careful to hide his surprise, Damien waited for her to say more.

"Of course, he isn't ruling that out. Apparently, diagnosing that sort of thing is pretty complicated. But he did say he leans more toward Borderline Personality Disorder."

"He didn't mention anything about this."

"Finn? Of course not. There's this little issue called doctor-patient confidentiality."

"Did he recommend any course of treatment?"

"Yep. He referred me to a psychologist up in Bozeman. I go once a week. I've gone twice so far."

He hugged her. "Did he give you any medicine?"

"Yep." Looking up at her brother, she smiled. "It took it a while to work, but I feel better now than I have my entire life." She made a motion with her hand, mimicking a mountain and a valley. "The ups and downs aren't as dramatic."

"Good for you, Maise. I'm really happy for you."

Moving toward the coffeepot, she glanced at Damien over her shoulder. "Now, you've just got to get your life in order, bro. Once you do, all the Coltons will be happy."

"Except for Darius," he reminded her.

"Except for Darius," she echoed. Looking sad. "I just wish things could be different for him."

"Me, too," Damien said, surprising himself. "Me, too."

Eve spent Monday morning unable to stop smiling. Despite having to clean up the mess the intruder had made, despite waiting for the glass company to show up and fix her window, she kept thinking about what Damien had let slip the night before.

He cared about her.

What that might mean, she wasn't sure. However, she was pretty certain they'd moved beyond the friends-with-benefits stage. She definitely had.

Her salon was closed that day, so after a cup of coffee and an English muffin, she tackled cleaning up the mess. She hoped to have her living room back in some semblance of order by lunchtime. Bonnie Gene had offered to help, but Eve really hadn't wanted her mother fussing with her things. Also, Eve felt that doing this herself might help her heal.

First, she worked on her poor, broken Christmas tree. Once she removed the damaged branches, the formerly stately fir took on a dejected and battered look.

Removing all decorations and garland from it, she vacuumed up pieces of tree and shards of broken ornaments, sorting what was left whole into neat piles on her coffee table.

When she'd finished, she turned the tree again, wondering if she could somehow make it look halfway presentable.

Finally she settled on facing the most broken part back against the wall and fluffing up what would now be the front. Plugging in the lights, she realized she only had to make a minor adjustment to those. Her ornaments were mostly destroyed, but she had a box of pine cones in her garage that she could use. With Christmas only a few days away, she didn't want to go buy new ornaments now, so she'd improvise.

While the pine cones were drying, she turned her attention to the rest of the room. She'd have to toss a few things that had gotten broken, and she'd have to buy a new lamp, but after cleaning her wall and erasing the warning, she felt she'd done all she could.

Her stomach growled. Glancing at her watch, she saw it was nearly noon.

Her cell phone chirped. Caller ID showed an unknown caller. Eve answered anyway. "Hello?"

"Ten thousand dollars," a distorted male voice said. "Deposited into your bank account or left on your doorstep, no questions asked, whichever you prefer. You'll receive this if you are successful in making him leave town."

Darius Colton. Though she didn't recognize the voice, who else could it be?

"What?" Though she felt she should have had some witty comeback, Eve was too stunned to do more than stammer. "Who is this?"

"Don't concern yourself with that," the voice snarled. "Do you want the money or not?"

She took a deep breath, trying to keep herself from shaking. "Don't call me again."

"Twenty-five thousand. That's my final offer."

"Are you crazy?" By now she was gripping the phone so tightly it hurt.

"Not crazy, just determined. I want Damien Colton gone by Christmas, and you'll have an early cash present."

She pressed the disconnect button without replying.

A moment later, she dialed Damien's number, heart still pounding.

"I'll be right there," he said, when she'd finished relaying the story. "Don't move."

He must have driven at twice the speed limit, because barely ten minutes had passed before he rang her doorbell. When she opened the door, he took one look at her face and pulled her into his arms.

"Get your coat. Let's go somewhere and have a cup of coffee."

Relieved, she nodded and went to get her jacket. "How'd you know that getting out of the house is exactly what I need?"

Instead of answering, he kissed her cheek.

Because it was after lunch and the donut shop had already closed, they chose the Corner Bar and Grill over the Honey-B Café. After all, it was "their" place.

"We have fresh-baked peach pie," the waitress told them as she led them to a booth. "Just out of the oven."

"Sounds lovely." Eve smiled at the girl. "I'll take a piece, along with a cup of decaf coffee."

"Just coffee for me," Damien said. "Regular."

After the server left, Eve leaned back in her chair. "Thanks for being so kind," she said.

"That's what friends do," he teased, though she couldn't read the emotion that darkened his eyes. "And anyway, what happened to you is my fault. I shouldn't have made you sit with me at the Christmas luncheon."

Friends. Oddly enough, his words made her want to cry. Damn hormones. Clearing her throat, she managed a smile and a nod as the waitress returned with her pie and their drinks.

"Mmm, pie." Though her appetite had deserted her, Eve picked up her fork and dug in. When she glanced up, Damien was watching her intently. Meeting his gaze actually made her chest hurt with physical pain.

Fool. Returning her attention to the pie, she made herself go through the motions. Fork to mouth, chew and swallow. Repeat. Though she was sure the peaches were delicious, she couldn't taste anything.

Once again, she'd fallen in love with a man who thought of her as a friend. And she had no one to blame but herself. After all, she'd set up the rules. Too bad she hadn't been able to live by them.

The waitress bustled up to the table, standing almost as if she was trying to block them from seeing the door.

"Don't look now," she muttered, leaning in close. "But Lucy Walsh just walked in."

Lucy Walsh was Mark Walsh's daughter. She'd once been Damien's girlfriend, before he'd gone to jail for supposedly killing her father. Mark had discovered their relationship and had, according to local gossip, gone ballistic, threatening Damien. Based on this story alone, a jury had convicted Damien of murder and sent him to prison.

These days, Lucy had a lot to deal with. Not only had she learned her father had been alive all these years without contacting her or anyone in the family, but she'd had to cope with his recent murder all over again.

Rumor had it that Lucy had believed Damien guilty and had never gone to see him in prison. Until Eve had been seen in public with him, most of Honey Creek also believed Damien had harbored both an unrequited love for Lucy and an acrid, bitter resentment.

Now it seemed everyone in the Corner Bar wanted to see how Damien would deal with this.

Wary, Eve glanced at Damien. She wasn't sure how she'd react if he showed signs of pining after Lucy. The waitress, too, watched him intently, no doubt hoping for a reaction.

Appearing both unaware and completely unconcerned, Damien simply lifted his cup and asked for a refill.

Crestfallen, the server walked off to get the coffeepot.

Then, to Eve's shock, Lucy herself came over to the table.

"Afternoon, Eve. Damien." A pretty girl, Lucy had a youthful attitude and style of dress that made Eve feel ancient and dowdy.

"Hey, Lucy." Damien smiled. "How have you been?"

Though Lucy glanced curiously over at Eve, she gave the appearance of being completely at ease. "I'm good. I noticed you both at the Christmas luncheon. Even though I couldn't make it up there to say hi, I was glad to see you two together."

It was on the tip of Eve's tongue to tell her they weren't together, but she merely nodded.

"Any news on the investigation?" Damien asked.

"Not so far." Everyone in town knew Lucy was very tuned in to the murder investigation. Some speculated it was to make up for being so ready to believe Damien guilty.

"Well, I won't take up any more of your time. Merry Christmas to both of you!" With a jaunty wave, Lucy moved off. As she went, everyone in the place alternated between watching her and eyeing Damien and Eve.

"Lucy and I made our peace a while ago," Damien said, again making Eve feel as if he'd read her mind. "We were both young and foolish. She lost her father and didn't know who to blame. End of story."

"I still can't believe the police haven't been able to find out who killed him. Of course, there were a lot of people who would want Mark Walsh dead."

"This time, I suspect they're being more careful." His

smile tinged with bitterness, Damien eyed her pie. "Aren't you going to finish?"

"No." Suddenly feeling queasy, she slid the plate toward him. "Help yourself."

Flashing her a grin, he picked up his fork and dug right in.

Funny how something so simple as sharing a piece of pie could seem so intimate, so homey. Dang, she was in deep.

Chapter 14

As she'd predicted, the women started dropping by Salon Allegra around ten o'clock Tuesday morning, about an hour after she opened and thirty minutes after her first shampoo and set. Arriving in small groups of two or three, they made no pretense of needing to get a haircut or being interested in purchasing styling products. Instead, they all wanted to know about Eve and Damien.

The first bunch, three elderly ladies from Bonnie Gene's quilting group, asked Eve point-blank, completely disregarding the fact that she was in the middle of a haircut.

Fortunately, Eve had prepared a standard, noncommittal response. "We're just good friends," she said, smiling a carefree smile.

By Tuesday afternoon, not only were her ankles swollen and her back aching, but she thought if one more person asked her about her relationship with Damien, she would scream.

At least she had her work to distract her. Traditionally, the week leading up to Christmas was busy for her little salon. This year was no exception, but as the days flew by, the steady stream of gossip-hungry visitors far eclipsed her appointments.

By Christmas Eve, they'd finally begun to taper off.

For years she'd made it a practice to work only half a day on Christmas Eve, and she had just finished her last appointment. Finally, she could close the shop up and go home, where she had a date with some mulled apple cider.

The phone rang, which, since she had no one else listed for the rest of the day, most likely meant someone wanted to schedule a rush appointment. This happened every holiday. Someone realized they needed highlights or a cut before church services or the big day and panicked.

"Salon Allegra," Eve answered. Nothing but silence from the other end. Wrong number? "Hello?"

As she was about to hang the phone up, a small sound, almost a cry, close to a gasp, made her freeze.

"Hello?" she said again. This time, instead of silence, someone sobbed. Then the voice—feminine and low—whispered an unintelligible phrase.

Every nerve standing on alert, Eve strained to hear.

Silence.

"I'm sorry? I didn't understand you." She kept her voice gentle and soothing. "I couldn't hear you. Please, what did you say?"

"Help me. Please, help me." And the phone went dead.

Slowly replacing the receiver, Eve tried to calm her pounding heart. Sharon Colton. It had to be her. She'd said her husband was trying to kill her.

Grabbing her cell phone, she dialed Damien. The call went immediately to voice mail, which probably meant he was out in the mountains checking on cattle. He'd said the ranch typically gave the hands half a day off on Christmas Eve, so they rushed to complete all their chores in the morning.

Pacing the confines of her small reception area, Eve eyed the phone as if she thought the handset might suddenly grow wings. For the first time ever she wished she had caller ID on her business phone.

What to do? Her choices were clear: she could do nothing or she could take a drive out to the Colton ranch and make sure Sharon was all right.

The thought of confronting an enraged Darius Colton was daunting. Then she realized she could call Wes Colton. And say what? That she'd had a mysterious phone call and she wasn't sure, but she thought it might be his stepmother and oh, by the way, his father might be trying to kill her.

He'd think Eve had lost her mind. No, thank you. Pacing, Eve tried to figure out a course of action—after all, she had her unborn baby to protect. Grabbing her parka, purse and car keys, she had just turned the sign on her door from Open to Closed when the phone rang again.

"Eve?" The voice sounded weak and wavery, but closer to normal. "This is Sharon Colton. I've had a bit of an accident with my hair."

"A bit of an accident?" Eve repeated. "What do you mean?"

Silence, then Sharon Colton answered, her voice low and full of pain. "Darius took scissors to it." Her breath caught in a sob. "I look a fright and I have to put in an appearance at the big caroling thing tonight. Can you come by and fix me up?"

Cautiously, Eve agreed. "Did you call a second earlier?"

After a moment's hesitation, Sharon admitted she had. "I'm sorry if I frightened you."

"You said 'Help me.'" Choosing her words carefully, Eve tried to figure out what to say. "Are you in need of some help?"

Another short hesitation, then Sharon said, "No."

"Is he there?"

"Darius?" Sharon gave a short laugh which ended in a hiccup. "No. He went down to his office."

"Are you hurt?" Eve persisted.

"You know what?" Sharon sighed. "I'm sorry I involved you in this. Forget I called."

She hadn't answered Eve's question.

"Wait, don't hang up. I'll come and fix your hair." Taking a deep breath, Eve tried to think. "That is, if it's safe for me to be there."

"Safe?" Weary impatience tinged Sharon's voice. "Of course it's safe. Why would he want to hurt you?"

Good question. Unfortunately, Eve kept seeing the rancor in Darius's stare. Still, the older woman needed help. "I can be out there in twenty minutes, all right?"

"Thank you. And I'm sorry to bother you on Christmas Eve. I'll double your usual tip for this."

"That's okay," Eve said. Hanging up the phone, she grabbed her parka, locked the door and headed out to her SUV.

An hour of her time doing a Christmas Eve favor to a woman she liked. What could be the harm in that?

Course decided, she headed out.

The drive out to the ranch took fifteen minutes. As she turned down the long driveway leading toward the main house, snowflakes appeared in her headlights. No flurries, these, but a steady, blanketing snowfall that carried the promise of becoming a storm.

Had the weathermen predicted this? She couldn't remember. In a matter of moments, the wind picked up and the snow started falling in earnest. Though snow was as common as cattle to Montana, snow on Christmas Eve was relatively rare. Magical.

Parking near the barn, she noticed the place seemed almost deserted, the ranch hands having been given the afternoon off so they could begin their holiday early.

Climbing from her SUV, she stood for a moment in the swirling snow, enjoying the crisp purity of the air, the cleansing beauty of the white curtain of snow. Then, she went to the house and rang the front doorbell.

No one came. She pressed the bell again and waited, but no one answered the door. Nerves prickling, she tried the handle, knowing it would be unlocked. Should she go inside or call Sharon on her phone to come let her in?

Remembering the humiliation in the older woman's voice, she decided to search her out on her own. Stepping into the huge marbled foyer, she closed the door behind her.

Wow. Awestruck for the space of a heartbeat, she gaped at the huge ranch house. Though her family was wealthy in their own right, the Coltons' ranch house was as different from the Kelley mansion as night and day. Though they were similar in size, there the resemblance ended.

Done in warm tones of oak and cedar, the Coltons' home exuded warmth and country living. The casual Western style reminded her of their state. Eve always thought Montana's true spirit was the unusually strong bond between the people, the animals and the land.

A huge evergreen tree dominated the great room, decorated in a rustic style that perfectly complemented the room's decor.

Inside, she circled the huge den, making her way into the kitchen, which was also empty. From there she went down a short, carpeted hallway, thinking it might lead to a guest bedroom or office of some kind.

As she rounded the corner, she heard Darius Colton's distinctive voice and froze, praying he wasn't about to hurt Sharon again.

"You know, I thought trashing the Kelley girl's place would make my son realize he needs to quit poking his nose where it doesn't belong, but no." Darius made a sound of disgust.

Eve crept closer. The older man stood in front of a wall of floor-to-ceiling windows, phone in hand.

"I agree. Though I hate to do it, I see no alternative. I'll have to kill him like I did Mark Walsh and that first guy, whoever he was." He chuckled. "Yes, I did just say I'd have to take out my own son. Hell, I made sure he got sent to prison, didn't I?"

He laughed, a malicious chuckle. "One good thing about him is that we can make it look like a suicide. Since he just got out of prison, I can claim he was having trouble making it on the outside."

Involuntarily, Eve gasped, the sound escaping her throat in a high-pitched squeak.

Darius turned. He pinned her with his gaze.

Oh, God. Eve took one step back, then another. She didn't hear what he said next, but he hung up the phone and moved swiftly toward her.

"Well, well." On his way toward her, Darius snatched up a heavy ceramic-and-brass lamp from his desk, ripping the plug from the wall.

Eve turned to run, aware she was far too late.

Darius grabbed her arm, yanking her feet out from under her. As she spun to face him, the last thing she saw was his arm raised, lamp in hand, before he hit her.

Though the Christmas carol sing wasn't slated to begin until dusk, Damien was rushing through his chores. Though the ranch hands had all been given leave to knock off work at noon, it was generally understood that all assigned chores must be completed, and Damien and one other man had driven bales of hay up into the pastures for the cattle and the horses. Each had taken a flatbed pickup with two huge round bales and spread the hay out for the animals' daily feed.

Though snow had started falling heavily, Damien completed his task, then returned to the ranch to park the truck next to several others in back of the barn.

At least three inches of snow had fallen during the time he'd been out in the pasture, blanketing the equipment and the vehicles. Though the parking lot in front of the barn had grown rapidly more deserted as ranch hands took off for town, a few remaining vehicles were covered in white snow, making them indistinguishable from their surroundings.

Back at the ranch house, Damien whistled as he washed up in the mudroom, before heading toward the kitchen to grab a quick snack.

Behind him, the back door blew open, slamming against the outside wall. He must have not closed it right. Frowning, he turned back around and came face-to-face with Darius, disheveled and covered in snow.

"What happened to you?" he asked, curious. In the entire three-plus months he'd been home, he'd never seen his father looking like this, not even at his drunken worst.

Instead of answering, Darius grunted something unintelligible and hurried away to his office, trailing snow and leaving tracks of mud.

The back of Damien's neck prickled. Something was wrong. Going against his better judgment, he followed his father.

Rounding the corner, he spied Darius, still wearing his coat, hurriedly picking up broken pieces of glass and china.

"What happened?" he asked, moving forward to help.

"Leave it alone," Darius snarled. "I'll get it. I broke my desk lamp."

"Out in the hallway?" Struck by an even stronger sense of trepidation, Damien moved closer. "What really happened here?"

"None of your damn business," Darius snarled. "If you know what's good for you, you'll get out of here."

Just then, Sharon Colton rounded the corner. Seeing her husband and her stepson, she froze, one hand to her mouth. Her left eye was swollen, raw and purple, and her mouth looked as though it had had a run-in with a fist.

"Did you hit her?" Damien asked, voice low and furious. "For the love of God, tell me you didn't hit your wife."

As he advanced on his father, Sharon gave a low cry.

Damien froze. Darius had produced a Smith and Wesson revolver and now had it pointed straight at him.

Eve came to slowly, wondering why she was so cold. Dang heater must be on the blink, which meant she needed to put in an emergency call to Rusty's Air Conditioning and Heating Service. She was trying to rise when the blinding pain in her head made everything spin.

What the...? Suddenly she remembered. Testing her arms, she found they were tied behind her back and she couldn't move them. The same applied to her legs. Darius

Colton had hit her with the lamp, knocking her out. Which meant she was…where?

Eyes adjusting to the darkness, she slowly looked around. She lay on a bale of hay, surrounded on three sides by other large rectangular bales. Since the huge round bales were used for the pastured livestock and these large squares were used to feed the barn-penned animals, she had to be close to the main barn. A hay barn, most likely.

Listening, she heard only silence, the heavy snowfall outside blanketing all sound. No livestock here, confirming her earlier guess.

She could only wonder what Darius Colton meant to do with her, especially since she'd overheard him not only confessing to a murder, but planning to have his own son killed.

Protectively cradling her stomach and the unborn life growing inside her, she began looking for a way out. Christmas Eve was a time for living, not dying. No way she would go out without a fight.

"What are you doing?" Damien asked, stopping in his tracks and eyeing the gun. Behind him, Sharon Colton began to cry, soft gasps of sound that barely drew the old man's attention.

"What I should have done months ago," Darius snarled. "You should have stayed in prison. Poking your nose around where you don't belong, just like your stupid girlfriend."

Damien's blood turned to ice. "Eve? What has she got to do with this?"

"I asked her to come out here and fix my hair," Sharon's broken voice answered. "I was just looking for her now."

Glaring at the man who'd sired him, Damien took a step forward. "What have you done with her?"

"Stay back."

"What have you done with her?"

Darius laughed. The guttural, malevolent sound sent a chill up Damien's spine.

He took a step closer. "Darius, what have you done to Eve?"

"Don't worry, I didn't kill her. Yet. Though with the storm raging outside, she may freeze to death before I have to. Rest assured, I will take care of her. Just like I'm going to have to take care of you."

Darius lifted the weapon, squinting at Damien as though he was about to fire.

"She's pregnant," Damien blurted, thinking fast. Back in the old days, before he'd gone to prison, his father had really cared about family and the Colton dynasty. "Eve is pregnant. You can't kill a pregnant woman."

This startled the older man. "Pregnant?"

"With my son," Damien lied, wishing with all of his heart that it was so. "Your grandson. Eve is carrying the next Colton."

For the first time a glimmer of humanity showed in Darius's flat, cold eyes. Slowly he lowered the gun.

Now! Damien moved, knocking the gun from his father's hands and slamming the older man into the floor.

"Where is she?"

Instead of answering, Darius struggled to free himself.

"Sharon, go call the police," Damien ordered, tightening his grip.

Wide-eyed, the woman stood frozen, staring at her stepson who had her husband wrapped in a choke hold.

"You will not," Darius rasped. "Sharon, get my gun and take this son of a bitch out."

Slowly, as though his voice compelled her, Sharon Colton moved toward the weapon.

"Bring me the gun and go and call Wes." Damien urged. "Do it now, Sharon, before anyone else gets hurt. We've got to try and find Eve. We've got to save her."

Shaking her head as if coming out of a trance, Sharon nodded. Turning, she went for the revolver first, handing it to Damien, who accepted it with one hand before pushing up and off his father.

Sharon then moved toward the office. She reached for the phone and started dialing, keeping a wary eye on her husband, who remained on the floor. Her single act of rebellion appeared to knock the remaining wind from Darius's sails.

A moment later, she returned to the hall. "Wes is on his way. And Jake Pierson is with him."

"Good." Damien liked Jake, who had been one of the first FBI agents to arrive in town. Since then, he'd left the Bureau and now he had a private security business and worked with Wes in the Sheriff's Department, intently focused on solving the Mark Walsh murder. If anyone deserved to find answers, Jake did.

"Where're Maisie and Jeremy?"

"At church. She volunteered to head up the organization for the Christmas carol sing this year."

"Good. I don't really want them to see this."

Keeping the gun trained on Darius, Damien backed away. "We've got to find Eve," he told his father's wife.

"If he left her somewhere outside, she won't last long in this weather."

"She's probably already dead." Darius sounded gleeful. "You may have won this round, but in the end, I've won the battle."

"What battle, Darius?" Sharon rounded on her husband. "You've alienated and injured your entire family, all in the pursuit of your business. I've lied long enough for you. I know where you keep the second set of books. Heck, I helped you set them up. I'm ashamed of that now. I'm going to turn in my CPA license, as soon as I turn those books over to the FBI."

"You wouldn't dare," Damien snarled. "Or I'll kill you, too."

Shaking her head, Sharon ignored him. "I'll go see if I can rustle up a search party. Don't worry, Damien, we'll find your girl."

With all his heart, Damien had to believe that. A moment later, Sharon returned.

"I got hold of Duke," she announced. "He's gathered up the ranch hands who were still here and they've split up into search groups."

"Good." He felt a sliver of the tension ease. He wouldn't feel anywhere near normal again until he held Eve in his arms. "I'll join them as soon as reinforcements show up."

In what seemed like an hour but was really only ten minutes, Wes and Jake arrived. Turning over the gun and Darius to his brother, Damien watched while Jake handcuffed the patriarch of the Colton Clan.

"How far the mighty have fallen," Jake muttered. "I've contacted several of my old coworkers in the Bureau. Most of them have gone home for Christmas, but they'll be back on the twenty-sixth to wrap part of this investigation up. Sharon's willingness to share the books and testify will help tremendously."

Damien nodded, barely hearing the other man. He ran for his parka, cramming his hat onto his head and shoving his fingers into gloves. "I'll be out searching. If you can get together more men to help search, I'd be grateful."

"They're already on their way." Wes clapped his brother on the shoulder. "Jake can keep an eye on Darius. Let's go."

"Wait," Darius cried as they turned to go. "I'll tell you where she is in exchange for my freedom."

"No." The two brothers spoke in unison. "No deals."

"Wes, Damien, you're my sons," Darius pleaded. "Let me go. I promise I'll disappear quietly. I'll sign over all this to you and you'll never hear from me again."

"Tempting as the offer is, we'll pass." Damien spoke through clenched teeth, knowing without asking that Wes felt the same way. Darius had bullied the family long enough.

Together, he and Wes headed out. At the doorway, Wes stopped.

"Are you sure you want to add murder to your list of crimes?" Wes asked quietly, turning to look at his father. "You have a choice here. You can tell us where Eve is and save her life, or you can let us search. If she dies, I'll make sure you're brought up on murder charges, do you understand?"

Instead of answering, Darius turned his face away.

"Come on, man." Damien took off, no longer caring if Wes was behind him. He barreled outside, into the midst of a blizzard.

"Damn." Wes came up beside him. "This got worse fast. On the way here, we had some visibility. Now it's whiteout conditions."

"I don't care." Damien started blindly in the direction of the cattle pens. "We've got to find Eve."

"I'll take the cattle pens," Wes told him. "You go check the machinery barn and the hay sheds."

Without another word, Damien turned and went the other way.

The angels of Christmas Eve must have been with him that night. Barely five minutes into his search, he pushed open the door of the hay barn and found Eve, trussed up and freezing, but alive and drifting in and out of consciousness.

Gathering her close, he freed her arms and legs, massaging them to bring circulation back, hoping she wouldn't have frostbite. She cried out in pain as feeling returned, violently shivering.

"Damien," she croaked, nearly unintelligible because of the shudders racking her body. "Darius killed Mark Walsh and the first guy, a homeless man that everyone thought was Mark Walsh. He let you go to prison knowing you were innocent. And now he was going to have you killed, I heard him."

"Shhh." Hushing her by placing one gloved finger against her mouth, he tried to determine the extent of her injuries. "We'll deal with that later, once we get you inside."

Then, lifting her, he carried her out into the snowstorm. When they reached the house, he carried her into the den, where he gently lowered her to the rug in front of the roaring fire.

Seeing her, Sharon wept with relief, heading into the kitchen and putting on a pot of hot water for tea. When she returned, Damien put her in charge of calling in all the searchers and letting them know Eve was safe.

With the Christmas tree shining brightly in the background, Damien crouched by the fire, helping Eve sip her tea and rubbing her legs, feet and hands, watching as her color slowly returned and her trembling subsided.

"You're safe now, sweetheart," he whispered, kissing her cheek. "I'll tell Wes what you heard."

Her beautiful blue gaze searched his face. "Are you all right? It must be a shock, knowing your own father wanted to kill you?"

"No worse than knowing he let me go to prison for a

crime he committed. But you're safe and that's all that matters."

Drowsily, she snuggled against him. Contentment filled his heart. He felt complete and at peace for the first time since he'd stood in that courtroom, fifteen years ago, and watched a prison sentence being handed down, sending him away for a crime he hadn't committed.

"I told them you were pregnant," he whispered into her hair.

"That's okay." Smiling, she kissed him. "It's about time I stopped worrying about tarnishing the family name."

"I, er, told them the baby was mine."

She froze, then turned in his arms to gaze up at him. "Why'd you go and do something like that?" she whispered softly. "It'll only make it worse when they find out the truth."

"Maybe they don't have to find out the truth." He kissed her lightly on the lips, then the nose, then the curve of her neck.

"What are you saying?"

Tightening his arms around her, he closed his eyes, inhaled her scent and took the leap. "Because I'd like that baby to be mine. He can be the first of our children, Eve. That is, if you'd like more."

"Damien?"

To his dismay her gorgeous eyes filled with tears, spilling over and trailing silver down her cheeks. Despair filled him as he realized he'd made her cry, which could mean only one thing.

She didn't want him.

"I'm sorry, I—" he began stiffly. "I didn't mean—"

"Don't you dare apologize, cowboy." Putting her arms around him, she kissed him full on the mouth. "That's the nicest thing anyone has ever said to me. But I need to know, are you suggesting we live together, or are you wanting to make an honest woman out of me?"

Hope slammed into him, hard, nearly making him gasp.

"You mean you'd marry me?"

Cocking her head, she gave a soft chuckle. "If you ask me right, I just might."

Slowly, he grinned. "How do you think your sister would feel about a double wedding? Her and Duke and me and you."

Eve's answering smile warmed his heart. "I guess we'll just have to ask her, now won't we?"

Epilogue

Valentine's Day dawned clear and cold, without a single cloud to mar the bright blue perfection of the sky.

The entire town of Honey Creek gathered at the town square, cameras in hand, ready to record the historical day.

Coltons and Kelleys, wed in a double ceremony. A joyous occasion which they hoped would go a long way toward erasing the shadow that had hung over their town for so long.

Though clearly ill, Darius Colton had gone to jail and was awaiting trial for the murder of Mark Walsh, as well as for the murder of the unknown drifter fifteen years ago. The twists and turns of this soap opera-like story had finally drawn the attention of the popular television show, *Dr. Sophie,* and they'd actually sent a camera crew to do an exposé on the scandal, much to Maisie Colton's delight. She'd even managed a cameo appearance. "The Scandal at Honey Creek," as their episode had been named, would air in the spring.

Eve Kelley's pregnancy had been announced, and though she'd refused to let Damien take responsibility for the baby, he made it clear to her that he'd be raising the child as his own.

Susan and Duke were jubilant when Damien and Eve had decided to marry, and this joint wedding would be the culmination of months of planning on Susan's part, one wedding easily stretched to become two, though she'd had to change the date slightly.

Sharon Colton remained at the ranch, finally emerging from her shell now that she was no longer under Darius's grip. She'd started a support group for battered women and traveled often to Bozeman, where she'd headquartered her office.

Church bells chimed the hour and a hush fell over the crowd. Finally, the sound of hooves on pavement filled the air. Two white, horse-drawn carriages turned the corner, decorated with white and peach roses, clattering down Main Street. The two brides, Susan and Eve, both decked out in ornate white gowns, rode in the first. The grooms, Duke and Damien, wearing matching gray tuxedos, followed in the other. They would arrive at the church, where the rest of the family and wedding party waited, seconds apart, and the ceremony would commence.

Because both Susan and Eve had wanted small weddings, the ceremony itself was by invitation only and had been limited to family and close friends. Later, everyone in town was welcome to attend the huge reception at the Colton ranch. The Rollaboys had been booked to play, Kelley's Cookhouse would be catering the reception, and the open bar provided by the Coltons ensured the celebrations would last long into the night.

Inside the church, two nervous brides prepared to walk up the aisle at the same time, sharing their father's arms. They knew two loving cowboys waited for them, both wearing identical looks of love on their handsome faces.

And Duke and Susan Colton, Damien and Eve Colton, were pronounced husband and wife. Both couples kissed sweetly.

When the ceremony was over, everyone lined the streets to watch them go past before racing to follow them. For the first time in recent history, the ranch house would be opened to the public, and the two newlywed couples would receive guests for two hours, before joining the party.

Despite the double wedding, the two couples were taking separate honeymoons. Duke and Susan were traveling to Jamaica and Damien and Eve had chosen Ixtapa, Mexico.

And when they returned, Damien would be moving to Eve's house. He'd agreed to continue to work on the ranch, side by side with the rest of his family.

He planned to persuade Eve to let him adopt her unborn child, giving him or her the Colton name. Once she'd agreed, which he had no doubt she would, he looked forward to good-naturedly needling all his brothers that he would have the first Colton baby. He had no doubt one of his brothers and their new bride wouldn't be far behind.

All in all, Damien planned to live a life full of happiness and love with his beautiful wife, Eve, and their baby. A normal life in the Big Sky Country, exactly as he wanted. Happily ever after. Of course.

* * * * *

COMING NEXT MONTH

Available December 28, 2010

ROMANTIC SUSPENSE

SRSCNM1210

REQUEST YOUR
FREE BOOKS!

2 FREE NOVELS PLUS 2 FREE GIFTS!

ROMANTIC
SUSPENSE

Sparked by Danger, Fueled by Passion.

HARLEQUIN®

A Romance

FOR EVERY MOOD™

Spotlight on

Classic

Quintessential, modern love stories
that are romance at its finest.

See the next page
to enjoy a sneak peek from
the Harlequin Presents® series.

*Harlequin Presents® is thrilled
to introduce the first installment of
an epic tale of passion and drama by*
USA TODAY *Bestselling Author*
Penny Jordan!

*When buttoned-up Giselle first meets
the devastatingly handsome Saul Parenti,
the heat between them is explosive....*

"LET ME GET THIS STRAIGHT. Are you actually suggesting
that I would stoop to that kind of game playing?"

Saul came out from behind his desk and walked toward
her. Giselle could smell his hot male scent and it was making
her dizzy, igniting a low, dull, pulsing ache that was taking
over her whole body.

Giselle defended her suspicions. "You don't want me here."

"No," Saul agreed, "I don't."

And then he did what he had sworn he would not do,
cursing himself beneath his breath as he reached for her,
pulling her fiercely into his arms and kissing her with all
the pent-up fury she had aroused in him from the moment
he had first seen her.

Giselle certainly *wanted* to resist him. But the hand she
raised to push him away developed a will of its own and
was sliding along his bare arm beneath the sleeve of his
shirt, and the body that should have been arching away
from him was instead melting into him.

Beneath the pressure of his kiss he could feel and taste
her gasp of undeniable response to him. He wanted to
devour her, take her and drive them both until they were
equally satiated—even whilst the anger within him that
she should make him feel that way roared and burned its

resentment of his need.

She was helpless, Giselle recognized, totally unable to withstand the storm lashing at her, able only to cling to the man who was the cause of it and pray that she would survive.

Somewhere else in the building a door banged. The sound exploded into the sensual tension that had enclosed them, driving them apart. Saul's chest was rising and falling as he fought for control; Giselle's whole body was trembling.

Without a word she turned and ran.

Find out what happens when Saul and Giselle succumb to their irresistible desire in

THE RELUCTANT SURRENDER

Available January 2011 from Harlequin Presents®

HPEXP0111

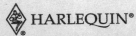

Love Inspired®

Bestselling author

JILLIAN HART

brings readers another heartwarming story
from

the
GRANGER
FAMILY
RANCH

To fulfill a sick boy's wish, rodeo star Tucker Granger surprises
little Owen in the hospital. And no one is more surprised than
single mother Sierra Baker. But somehow Tucker ropes her heart
and fills it with hope. Hope that this country girl and her son
can lasso the roaming bronc rider into their family forever.

Look for

His Country Girl

*Available January
wherever books are sold.*

www.SteepleHill.com

Steeple
Hill®

LI87643